Praise

Stories of Little Women and Grown-Up Girls:

"The book alternates between tears and an ironic smile, and between elegiac intonation and delicious touches of buffoonery typical of the previous book. We cry with the prisoner in 'Like in Jail' and we laugh satisfied (especially women) with the lesson the cello professor gives her accommodating lover in 'The Eighth Fold.'"
—*Hoy* (New York)

"Sonia is at war with the traditional and still dominant forms with which feminine subjectivity is represented in a patriarchal culture. Her alliance with emerging forms of the feminine (the nomad, the mestiza . . .) converts her into the traveling companion of many other creators and thinkers that, through history, literature, the visual arts, philosophy or political activism, are tracing a radically new map of the world of women."
—Marta Sofía López, Universidad de León (Spain)

"The stories of women that Sonia Rivera-Valdés presents keep this writer among the Hispanic talents who place the literary work of Latino writers of this city in the top echelon of originality, talent, and sincerity."
—*Siempre* (New York)

"With the particular charm of characters that could be any neighbor in El Barrio, and the attractive turbulance of some stories that capture attention and teach in endearing ways, Sonia Rivera-Valdés performs a service to literature, to the elastic gay-lesbian-queer community of the Hispanic world, to groups discriminated against or marginalized by local supremacies, and to all of us who believe in the dignity of the human being and in the value of differences."
—Susana Reisz, Lehman College (New York)

"The stories are constructed by an image that destabilizes all attempts at clear and precise definition; their aesthetic conspires against all processes of institutionalization or naturalization of accepted limits. . . . What characterizes these stories are not their stereotypical nature, but rather their constant crossing of the lines of accepted codes, their insistent questioning of the limits imposed by stereotypes."
—Emilio Bejel, author of *Gay Cuban Nation*

"Sonia Rivera-Valdés has set out to search for a language, for a kind of writing, that would subvert the model, and along the way has created believable and functional characters, narrators, and narrations. She resorts to irony and parody when needed to enhance meaning, but above all she has avoided the deceptive reflection of the stereotypical and untruthfully Caribbean. She has neither trivialized the narrative voice, that of her characters, nor that of the author herself, and has succeeded in not letting the model die behind the mask of a fictitious construct labelled 'Caribbeanism.'"

—Alicia Perdomo, City University of New York

"I sat on the bed to listen to myself with a book as interlocutor. At around page fifty, tears surprised me, and I gave myself over to the accumulated pain. . . . Thank you for *Stories of Little Women and Grown-Up Girls*."

—Anna Chover, Valencia University (Spain)

"When I finished reading *Stories of Little Women and Grown-Up Girls* I remembered what Luce Irigaray said about eastern philosophy because these stories are exactly the opposite. Instead of formulating the real, removing it from concrete experience, her writing makes us stronger and wiser, more able to face life itself."

—Margarita Drago, author of *Memory Tracks: Fragments from Prison (1975–1980)*

"The book is a kind of emotional x-ray of a series of women who, in trying to accommodate as much as possible both their lives and their desires, reflect on the stories that have touched them, the ones they have chosen, lived, and faced without fear, and that until now have been their destiny."

—Paquita Suárez Coalla, author of *Mi vida ye una novela*

Praise for Sonia Rivera-Valdés' previous works:

"Vastly entertaining, slyly heretical, and probably the most important book of stories since Joyce's *Dubliners*."
—William Monahan, author of *Light House*

"The mad, the curious, the inexplicable in human behavior—that which is not sanctioned by society—are the pivotal points in Sonia Rivera-Valdés' narratives. Her characters live fully, without misstep, precisely because the author has turned the tables on propriety."
—Zaida Capote,
Institute of Literature and Linguistics (Cuba)

"Revelatory." —*Library Journal*

"Sonia Rivera-Valdés presents a prose that is unconstrained, daring, reminiscent of Anaïs Nin."
—*Oh! Magazine* (Dominican Republic)

Stories of Little Women
& Grown-Up Girls

Sonia Rivera-Valdés

Translated by Emily Maguire

Editorial Campana

NEW YORK

Copyright © 2007 by Sonia Rivera-Valdés
Translation copyright © 2005 by Silverwind Productions, Inc.

Originally published in Spanish as
Historias de mujeres grandes y chiquitas, by Editorial Campana,
copyright © 2003 by Sonia Rivera-Valdés.

First English Edition, May 2007

All rights reserved. No part of this book may be used or reproduced in any manner whatsoever without written permisson except in the case of brief quotations embodied in critical articles and reviews.

Editorial Campana
19 West 85th Street
New York, NY 10024
www.editorialcampana.com

Library of Congress Cataloging-in-Publication Data
Rivera-Valdés, Sonia.
Stories of little women and grown-up girls / Sonia Rivera-Valdés ;
translated by Emily Maguire.
p. cm.
ISBN-13: 978-0-9725611-6-7
ISBN-10: 0-9725611-6-1
1. Rivera-Valdés, Sonia--Translations into English. I. Maguire, Emily,
1976- II. Title.
PQ7079.2.R55A2 2006
863'.64--dc22
2006038021

Book design by Phoebe Hwang
Jacket design by Yolanda V. Fundora

Printed in the United States of America

9 8 7 6 5 4 3 2 1

For the women who, like Ana Messeguer with her story of the moon and her fear of sleeping alone as a child, told me an anecdote about themselves or someone else, or said something, sometimes without intending to, that took root inside me and grew until it became one of these stories.

In the case of the four tales inspired by the life and death of Ana Mendieta, I want to state clearly that I woud have changed them without wavering, had I had the chance, to avoid having to erase her name and address from my address book.

Without Jorge Luis, Marito, Chuchi, Pepe, and their families, Jacqueline, Margarita, Paquita, Vivian, Juana, Hilda, Nereida, Betty, and Daisy, this book would not exist.

Contents

Necessary Note	11
Ana at Four Times	
Ana and the Moon	14
Ana and the Magic Wand	22
Ana and the Snow	41
Ana and the Lemon Balm	57
Like in Jail	69
The Eighth Fold	79
Sunday at the Same Time	92
Blue Like Bluing	98
The Deepest Seed of the Lemon	129
Life Leads	150
About the Author and the Translator	173

Necessary Note

A promise is a debt; wait a little bit, my mother would assert in her florid Andalusian accent on those rainy Havana afternoons, as an answer to my insistence that she stop filling a tray with *torrejas* to offer to some neighbor tempted by the fame of her desserts. Once the sweets were submerged in their anise-scented syrup, she would sit down to tell me about her childhood in a small town, where there was more than enough space for games. Her stories were my favorite pastime. The only open fields I ran through were the ones she had run through as a child, the only trees I climbed were the sturdy oaks of her memories, where, crouched on their trunks, she evaded maternal discipline countless times and where, four months before I was born, she watched from one of the highest and most fragile branches, paralysed with fear, as a group of police officers murdered my father.

Here are the *Stories of Little Women and Grown-Up Girls* that I promised to publish during my conversation, now some years ago, with Marta Veneranda del Castillo Ovando. With the conclusion of this project, I am paying various debts, the most pressing, for me, to Ana Mendieta, the Cuban sculptor who died tragically in 1985 at age thirty-seven. "Ana at Four

Times" is not an attempt to present a chronological recounting of her life. It presents key moments of her fragmented existence that I have tried to charge with her passion for life, with her spirit, with her emotion, with her way of seeing and feeling the world. Perhaps I should say, what *I* perceived to be her way of seeing and feeling the world.

I hope this story reflects how much I valued her friendship, admired her as an artist, and mourned her premature death.

I hope that Marta Veneranda, a close friend since our interview when she was collecting her forbidden stories, will enjoy "The Deepest Seed of the Lemon," a version of the anecdote that I told her that she then turned into her celebrated story, "The Most Forbidden of All." I trust that she won't be offended by my mentioning her in "Life Leads," since I truly respect her. Besides, something has happened with this story that I consider to be one of those "little miracles" that Carmina, the protagonist of "Blue Like Bluing," another story in this volume, talks about.

Paquita Suárez Coalla, a dear friend and one of the first people to read my manuscripts, gave birth to a daughter on July 8, 2001, and named her Jacinta, the same name given to that granddaughter of yours whose existence you found out about after I met her during a trip to Cuba. I wrote the story almost two years before Paquita became pregnant, when she couldn't even imagine that she would pick such a beautiful—and, at the time, unusual—name for a daughter who at that moment didn't even form part of her plans. Imagine the joy of Marta Eugenia, mother of the Cuban Jacinta, when she learned that there was another little girl with that name in New York. She had commented to me that she knew no one in Havana who had thought about giving their child that name, and that her decision had provoked more than a little criticism. Remembering the story of when my mother decided to name me Martirio, and the stories of Marta Eugenia and Obdulia, there in Havana, I understood.

Those who have read *The Forbidden Stories of Marta Veneranda* will recognize the strong influence of those stories on "Life Leads," the last story in this volume. My imitation of that model is my way of thanking its author for having helped me process, if involuntarily, that bitter tale that had so controlled me.

Martirio Fuentes
New York
July 12, 2001

Ana at Four Times

For Ana Messeguer

ANA AND THE MOON

Ana was already five years old, and there was no way that she was going to get used to sleeping by herself. Night after night she could be heard protesting the trip to bed. The problem was not falling asleep. Once they got her to lie down, she was out immediately, as long as there was no light on. It was the waking up in the morning, the pounding of her heart, and the sweating. That was what she feared. On her feet in one jump, her completely round eyes wide open, she ran, although only a few steps separated her from her parents' room, and, to the beat of cries whose anguished tone drove the whole house to its feet, threw herself against the closed door. Three or four times a week, always before five in the morning.

"As if she were running from some terrifying nightmare," the adults commented at breakfast, ignoring her presence, and she listened without responding or raising her eyes from the glass of chocolate milk she abhorred. Why didn't they serve her *café con leche* like everyone else? "Because children don't drink coffee, princess." "That's not true, and I'm not a princess." "Why isn't it true? What child have you ever seen drink coffee?" Ana would fall silent; she would never betray Domitila.

No, it wasn't that she had bad dreams; it was that she woke up. She never slept straight through till morning, not even as a baby, according to her mother, and on trying to see what was around her without being able to, her heart began to thump in her chest and grow larger. It felt big, heavy like one of the *guanábanas* that fell from the tree in the patio. She repeated this explanation, panting and winded, on various occasions when her parents opened their door for her, and everyone found the comparison of her palpitations to fruit so funny that they began to question her just to hear the tale again. They couldn't hide their smiles, even if they didn't mean to make fun of her. When Ana realized the real intent of their questions, her emotions tangled themselves up in the worst way, becoming a knot of fear, anger, and shame. She didn't answer any more.

The riddle that her trouble with sleeping posed for her family seemed unsolvable. The darkness terrified her, and the logical solution of leaving a light on in the room didn't work. The light made her open her eyes when she had only been asleep for ten minutes. Untiring during the day, she usually went to bed so sleepy that five minutes of a story from Domitila were enough to put her to sleep. They tried a votive candle, the smallest, to see if it could shine without bothering her. Ana still couldn't see, there was too little light, and the fear of a fire ruled out the candle when one night in her wildness to run to her mother, the child bumped into the glass containing the candle. The stuffed animal she clutched fell onto the flame and its feet were charred, despite their banging it against the tile floor to put it out before it was destroyed.

Ana sat through three sessions with a child psychologist, highly recommended, and not only refused to speak about her nighttime terrors, but refused to even open her mouth during the three visits. The therapist never heard the sound of her voice. At the end of the third visit, he gave a note to the driver they had sent for Ana, advising her mother to save the money they were paying him.

After calming her down, they would make her return to her room. Taciturn, she would go back down the small hallway accompanied by her mother. Alone again, sitting on her bed, she would squeeze her mouth shut to quiet the uncontrollable sobs that made her chest rise and fall. And with her face and eyes scrunched up, she would swallow the tears that she caught on her tongue as they fell, sticking the tip out of the corners of her mouth, first on one side, then on the other. Her whimpers would become stronger each time she thought of their morning jokes. She felt her heart among thorns now, crouched, and the sensation was so vivid that she unbuttoned her pajama top to touch her healthy body. Soaked in sweat, she made out the confusing silhouette of an old picture, a copy of a famous painting, in front of her bed. If she looked to the side, beyond the open door she could make out the grand piano in the living room on which she reluctantly practiced her lessons when she came home from school. During the day she detested the painting and the piano; at night they filled her with terror.

After many conjectures, no one could explain Ana's nighttime terrors, and the fact that she was the only daughter of a mother with no possibility of becoming pregnant again granted her the privilege of not being contradicted. Not even when she chose as a bedroom a room on the ground floor of the house, refusing to stay in her room on the upper floor and forcing her parents to abandon their spacious room to move to a smaller one next to hers. Her parents humored Ana without comment, hopeful of having peaceful dreams, even at the cost of the beautiful view of the *flamboyán* tree they had enjoyed before. The scenes continued below; if not with greater intensity, as that was impossible, at the same level. On seeing the uselessness of the move, her parents made an effort to convince her to return to her own room, so that they could recover their own comfort. They redecorated her room. Against her own taste, her mother even picked out a bedspread printed with violet flowers, Ana's favorite color, and a matching bed skirt. "And what a purple. It's the color of an old lady's clothes, the color of Holy Week." Not even then. Her disconcerting attitude (because after three or four mornings of little smiles at breakfast, on finishing her story of the fear from the night before, there was no way to make her open her mouth to say how she felt) did not change until the arrival of Aunt Clemencia, early one Saturday, from Miami.

She was unknown to Ana; they hadn't seen her for ten

years. A stubborn arthritis that gave her little mobility in her knees made it difficult for her to climb stairs and obliged them to give her the room that Ana occupied on the ground floor. They had to transfer the child—firm in her decision, on being consulted, not to sleep upstairs "even if they killed her"—to the seamstress's room, tiny and at the end of the long hallway, quite far from her parents' room, but the only available space on the ground floor. Ana, contrary to what they had foreseen, did not object to the change; and since her conduct was so often incomprehensible, they didn't even question her. On going to sleep, each member of the family did so terrified, predicting a torment of incalculable proportions.

Sunday morning, everyone was already in the dining room, ready to sit down at the table and anxious to comment on the strangeness of the previous night: not even a chaotic awakening, not even a cry. The little girl entered smiling; she didn't say good morning because she never did, but she sat down next to Aunt Clemencia, with her face washed and her teeth brushed, hair combed—unusual at such an early hour unless Domitila got her ready to go to school—and drank her chocolate milk without saying a word.

Ana had reasons for each one of her decisions. She refused to sleep upstairs because her room was right next to Aunt Ernestina's, and the combination of the early morning songs of her aunt's birds and the barking of the Pekinese bothered her. Now downstairs, she accepted the room change happily because when Aunt Clemencia (her great-aunt since she was the older sister of Matilde, Ana's dead maternal grandmother) arrived, Ana followed her to the room that would be hers for a few days. She watched her as Aunt Clemencia unpacked and placed into a drawer of the chest they had set aside for her a great quantity of fabric remnants in red, blue, yellow, bright green, some printed and several in a purple color, folded carefully. And she knew, because she had seen them, that she had brought colored thread, buttons, scissors. On noticing Ana's attentive gaze, the woman explained that they were for making rag dolls, and that the nanny who had cared for her as a little girl, the daughter of an African woman who had come to Cuba as a slave, had shown her how to make them.

Without the woman's knowing it, that short conversation established a strong bond between her and the little girl. It was the first time that she had heard someone in her own family talk to her like Domitila did.

"If you want, I can make you one tomorrow. And if you like, this week while I'm here I can make another each day; I love to make them. I sell them in Miami. People really like them. I can sew Monday, Tuesday, Wednesday, and so on, up to Sunday on their dresses, and you'll have a special one for each day of the week."

Ana couldn't believe it; someone was going to make a doll in front of her, a doll that she could play with, and she would know what it had inside, how they had shaped the nose, how they had made the eyes. Incredible. She had a lot of dolls, even a Mariquita Pérez doll, brought from Spain, that she was only allowed to play with after four in the afternoon, when she was already bathed and fed. Many times they had tried to get her to sit on a chair in the hall and rock Mariquita. She never did.

"A more poorly behaved child you couldn't have gotten if you'd asked," said Ernestina each time Ana refused, and the fine toy remained in the place set aside for her in a glass case until grandmother Teresa died, after the rest of the family had left the country. A few months after her death, the mansion became the headquarters of a cultural organization, and no one ever found out what then became of the doll.

But no one had made her a doll, not even Domitila. Domitila told her very good stories, made her cookies and cakes, but not dolls.

Ana thought all of this without making a sound, but she smiled at her aunt and nodded her head on hearing her proposal.

That night she didn't cause any trouble at bedtime, but she woke up earlier than usual, at two, perhaps due to her desire for dawn to arrive so that Clemencia could fulfill her promise. Disoriented, she opened her eyes, she sat up in bed, and instead of the darkness common at that hour, she was enveloped by a brilliant white light. Through the window facing the bed shone the moon. Ana watched it fixedly. Round, it resembled a huge, friendly face, someone she had known for a long time and in whom she could trust. She thought about Domitila. She looked at the ceiling, looked at the black and white floor tiles, the sewing machine on one side of the bed, surprised at her ability to see. She observed each object around her. The brightness allowed her to make out the details. Curious, she got up and walked around the room, surprised at the precision with which she could guide herself towards the furniture and touch their adornments, helped by the gentle light. She could even make out the hands of the clock on the nightstand perfectly. From her bed, she contemplated the heavenly body for a long time as she breathed in the scent of the lemon balm in the flowerpots that rested against the window. She had never before noticed how much the moon shone, nor noticed the scent of the lemon balm.

With great surprise, she woke up in her bed.

The week that Clemencia stayed there, Ana spent her middays in the small room with her aunt, helping her to put together the dolls, choosing cloth for dresses from among dozens of remnants and colors for eyes from a special jewelry box full of buttons whose lid, embroidered in sequins, read "Eyes for Dolls."

A little after nine, she would walk towards the moon room, since it was no longer the seamstress's room to her. The perfume from the flowerpots and the night through the open window lulled her to sleep. She learned that although the moon changed its shape and became smaller, it still kept her company, and when the sky was darker it was easier to see the stars, which to the little girl were small moons.

When Clemencia returned home, Ana refused to go back to the room next to her parents', refused to let them take the sewing supplies out of the room to put in a desk for her, and was never again afraid to sleep alone. No one asked her the reason for the change, and she never explained. Her mother knew that it had something to do with the moon, and attributed it in a vague way to the depth and darkness of Scorpio, Ana's sign. Everyone felt so relieved that they thought it was almost a miracle, and they were afraid to break the spell with words.

ANA AND THE MAGIC WAND

That year Ana asked the Three Kings for something very special, a magic wand. Like every Sunday, she had gotten up early, although neither her mother nor Grandma Teresa nor Aunt Ernestina understood why a seven-year-old girl would get up at dawn when she didn't have to go to school. Her father didn't concern himself with these things. She liked to watch the birds land on the big tree in the patio and hear them sing without anyone to interrupt them, and this only happened in the first hours of the morning, before Ernestina's Pekinese came down from the room on the second floor where she slept. Her barking made the birds fly away. At first Ana cried and insisted that Ernestina not let the dog out until the birds had left, but when her aunt said, "In any case, my canaries sing more prettily and one can hear them at any hour, without interrupting the poor dog or getting up at dawn," she easily convinced the other adults in the household that Ana's desires were pure nonsense.

"It's not the same," Ana answered, but at seven she lacked the words to express that she liked the birds in the patio for their freedom. They came when they wanted, sang as long as they wished to, and left for who knew where exactly when they felt like it. She followed them with her gaze until she could see the last straggler lose itself behind a far-away cloud. Afterwards she seated herself under the big tree, and with her eyes open, dreamed different dreams. Her favorite was the one in which she awoke one morning while everyone in the house was still asleep and went to the patio to observe the birds as always. But when the birds took flight, she would open her own blue and gold wings that had sprouted while she watched them, wings just like the ones on the little angels on the stamps they gave her in catechism class, and she would fly after the flock, following it from a certain distance, because she would need help to orient herself in the sky.

She was almost always shaken from this dream by the voice of her mother, calling her to breakfast. She reluctantly stood up and walked slowly towards the dining room, looking neither at the path nor the house, eyes downward, but her gaze turned in towards herself, where there was still the brilliant reflection of her wings in flight, illuminated by the sun. She stepped lightly, always over the same footprints. To vary the route made her afraid of she knew not what. A small error in a step, a slight deviation from her course and she was obliged to return to the bench and start out on the walk again. Sometimes there were days with two, three, even four attempts. On the grass could be seen the wake left by the small feet of the quiet little figure, who never left her state of absorption, even when she heard that mysterious pronouncement from her mother after running into the doorjamb of the door to the dining room:

"That child lives on the moon."

In reality Ana liked to talk, and she did it with Domitila and with herself when she was alone. It embarrassed her that her words provoked a laugh from the grown-ups; she still remembered their little smiles during the time when she was afraid to sleep alone, and frequently, on finishing her story, her mother affirmed with a smile,

"The things that happen to you." And later the little girl heard her story repeated to visiting friends of the family, when other topics of conversation had been exhausted.

The grown-up people in the house talked about things very far from Ana's interests. In general, they occupied themselves with the day's activities and with what they thought of doing in the coming days. At the dinner hour, her father commented on the current political events, and her mother and grandmother exchanged the latest news regarding family and friends, adding to each bit of news their opinion about what had happened. This exchange of information frequently provoked arguments, the product of different interpretations of stated facts. They argued while they ate, not paying attention to Ana's face, which would begin to lose its expression as the voices grew louder. The dispute would be momentarily interrupted by the little girl's cries: "My soup has gotten muddied," she would exclaim with her eyes open wide, although there was no soup in front of her. Her mother and grandmother would abruptly become quiet, looking at her strangely, and after some moments of silence that followed the dialogue, the two would begin to speak at the same time, each excusing herself for how nervous she had made the child, and if her father and Ernestina were present they would accuse them both. They would give her a glass of water and an ephemeral peace would reign.

In spite of the repetition of the enigmatic phrase, shouted

each time there were fights at the table, the arguments did not cease, forcing Ana to put up with them during her childhood until her parents moved to Miami. Once the verbal altercations were over, everyone silently asked themselves where Ana could have gotten the expression about her soup becoming cloudy. But once the storms were calm no one mentioned them, even if they were not resolved, and they never asked the child, whose conduct no one understood and each explained in a different way.

"It's unfortunate that she's inherited so much from her father's family," said her mother.

"Unfortunately, her personality much resembles that of her mother's family," Grandmother Teresa affirmed with authority.

For her part, Ana, since she never obtained an answer to the questions she asked, or because the answers didn't relate to the question, had created her own explanations for an indecipherable reality behind the words and had learned to resolve problems that overwhelmed her, like the arguments at the table, in her own way. She didn't invent; she only took the material overheard at the table and not understood and organized it in her head in accordance with a logic of her own. On various occasions, she heard her mother and grandmother say, speaking of some family trouble:

"This is a muddy topic, let's change the subject."

Another day she heard:

"Their relationship became muddied after the cousin arrived. It's best not to talk about it."

She thought that muddy and muddied were sounds that were necessary to follow with silence, and so she began to use these words when the adults argued, combining them with soup because she loved this dish. She never asked what they meant, because when the adults became buried in their conversations they never paid her the attention she required, not even to respond to questions about language. Or, even worse, they looked at her fiercely when she interrupted them.

She abandoned the habit of asking the day that she tried to find out what an *abortion* was. It was when she heard first her Aunt Clara and then a friend of her mother's say that they were going to have one. Ana's question received in reply the disapproving silence and accusing gaze that had been directed to her on other occasions, this time with more force. "I shouldn't have asked," she thought, but she had already done so. When they answered her, it was in a curt way that left no room for reply. It was a grown-up thing; she would find out when she was older.

She sat down on the patio to think, repeating the word ceaselessly with her lips closed until the sound, now bereft of unity, resonated disintegratedly in her ears, with sliding stress marks: a-bor-tion, á-bor-tion, a-bor-tión. Since she always heard the word come from the mouth of a woman in distress, she concluded that it had to do with something horrible that happened to them. The worst thing was that from this definition there followed the horrifying conviction that it was something that happened to all women, including her mamá and she herself when she grew up. From then on, she awaited with terror the arrival of the frequent days when her mother's face was somber, thinking that the sadness whose cause she did not understand was perhaps due to an abortion.

When those mornings arrived, she would run crying inconsolably through the patio, through the backyard and the stable, and take refuge where the house's land ended in the area set aside for target practice, to the surprise of the grownups, who would try without success to coax her out of her sorry state with candies and promises to take her to the movies. In the end, Domitila would bring her back to the house by promising her that they would make *croquetas* together.

No one noticed that family sadnesses occupied a large part of Ana's existence and that if she didn't want to go to bed when her father was not home by bedtime (even though after Clemencia's visit she no longer suffered the terrible nighttime worry that had plagued her before her aunt's stay), it was because she was terrified of waking up the following day with the suspicion that he had not returned during the night. Because if he hadn't, Mamá would wake up with her eyes red and almost swollen-shut, and Ana would be sure that she had cried a great deal. When this happened, the little girl left early and quietly for her refuge at the bottom of the back patio. She always returned to the house with a stomachache; they thought that she was feigning her upset stomach, and her grandmother made her go to school whether she was sick or not.

Ana's confusion grew when the morning following one of those subterranean storms she recognized, everyone sat down to eat breakfast with their customary smiles and their conversations about daily events. The simple mention of an event capable of darkening the family past provoked a sudden shift in conversation, and the sorrows of the present only appeared in her mother's tearful eyes, her grandmother's bad-tempered expressions, Aunt Ernestina's ironic ones, or her father's grim face. The silence closed off any possibility of airing deep sorrows or old grudges, of which there were frequent signs.

In the same way that Ana suspended her questions about the meaning of words, she gave up investigating why the grownups sometimes acted in ways that were incomprehensible to her. She learned this the day she came home from school before the usual hour, went to find Zuleika in her room so they could play, and on opening the door found her father on top of the girl. Zuleika was very young, she hadn't been serving in the house for very long, and she and Ana would play in the afternoons.

On registering the girl's presence, the bodies on the bed remained in the same position, as if the life had suddenly left them. Ana, leaning against the doorway, remained motionless, and although it was May she felt the same chill down her back as when a cold wind blew in January. She tried to run, but her feet wouldn't lift her off the ground, tried to close her eyes but, obstinate, they remained open, fixed on the scene that she couldn't bear to see. She began to sweat, her face burned, and her heart sounded in her throat and her ears. Two, three minutes passed, and suddenly a meteorite streaked off towards her grandmother's room. She didn't even think of asking her mother, whom she knew would have been too hurt by what she had seen. Besides, Teresa was her father's mother, and she knew about all the family business.

She arrived at the second floor sweaty and with a chill on her back. She swallowed saliva and asked, tripping over the words, with a great need to understand, for an explanation that would put her upside-down world in order. Her grandmother listened and didn't seem surprised. In a low voice, she told Ana that she shouldn't worry and should forget what she had seen, that she would speak to her son. She promised her that it wouldn't happen again, and warned her not to mention the incident because it could cause big problems.

Ana didn't mention it. Even without the warning she wouldn't have mentioned it, but she stopped kissing her papá when he came home from work. Her mother couldn't understand the reason for her behavior and insisted that she change it; the little girl refused and was punished by not being allowed to watch television for a week. Her grandmother, as was her habit, didn't consult anyone before lifting the punishment on the second day. However this time her mother defended her position, saying that it was one of the few times that she had decided to punish Ana with any severity. She was unusually surprised at her mother-in-law's resistance to the punishment, because the old woman had a marked inclination towards firm discipline with children. They argued, and, as usual, Teresa imposed her will. Her papá continued to bring Ana her favorite sweets and to call her princess. The only change in his conduct was that he intervened even less in decisions regarding his daughter.

The impact of that scene was so strong that her father's impassivity made her doubt that she had seen what she had. Maybe it had been a nightmare. Little by little the image of Zuleika's room grew hazier and she began to kiss her papá again when he returned from work, although something still worried her when she got close to him.

A dream brought her relief. A large eye, larger than any real one, an eye that was just eye, without a face and without a head. She held it in her two hands so that it wouldn't slip and pressed hard with her thumbs on each side of the pupil to squeeze the center. Small animals, deformed and gelatinous, in varying shapes, long and thin, round, with jumpy eyes and no mouth, began to come slowly out of it. Ana grabbed them as soon as they appeared and sat them on a chair. Just as she sat the last one down, Domitila entered the room with a bottle of disinfectant in her hand and sprinkled them with it. They died squished together. "Don't worry," said Domitila, "They won't bother you any more."

What she had dreamed seemed so real, and the scene she had witnessed days ago in Zuleika's room so far away, that the dividing line between reality and dream was almost erased. In the future, when thinking about these images it was very difficult to distinguish which realm corresponded to which memory.

In reality, Ana had two reasons for getting up early on Sunday. The first was the birds and the second was that on that day she and Domitila had coffee together, even though her mamá had forbidden the little girl to drink it. It was the first thing that she did before going to the patio. They drank it in the kitchen, seated at the rough wooden table where the old woman chopped onions, crushed garlic, and ate. She too got up every day to watch the sun rise, even when it was Sunday like today, and the eve of Three Kings Day.

The coffee and Domitila's stories were secrets shared, and they connected Ana to the cook more than the innumerable bottles that Domitila had fed her on her lap and the long hours that she had taken care of her when she was a baby. On those mornings, the old woman told stories about her family and explained the world. Contrary to the owners of the house, she *did* talk about her family sadnesses. Ana liked what Domitila told her so much that she made her repeat it over and over again. So, on various mornings, she talked about her small cousin that had disappeared many years ago just after being born, in mysterious circumstances.

One of the cook's aunts had more children than she could afford to care for when she found herself pregnant again. For nine months she cried, cursing her sorry luck and the husband that had made the child only to abandon her afterwards. The birth occurred at an hour in which all of the family was at work. Only Domitila, who at age ten had already left school to take over the household chores, was there. After bringing the midwife who always assisted her aunt, the girl sat down in a small room next to the bedroom where her aunt was in labor to await the birth. An hour later she heard the cry of a baby. She jumped up from the chair smiling and ran to the room to see it. The midwife blocked the doorway and ordered her to wait. After what seemed a long time to the girl—although now as an adult she thought that perhaps it wasn't such a long time, the midwife opened the door and let her in. The woman who had recently given birth looked very tired; she didn't open her eyes or speak as her niece entered. The baby, the midwife said, had been born dead, strangled by its own umbilical cord. It wasn't there. The two women seemed so worn out, the room so gloomy, that Domitila slipped away, regretful of having entered, and it was not until years later, when her aunt was no longer alive, that she mentioned the child's cry.

The first time that Ana heard the story, she asked the old woman why she hadn't said something. Domitila answered, looking her in the eyes,

"Because then everyone would have known that the child was born alive."

"Why did they lie to you? Where was it?" the girl asked, opening her eyes.

"I don't know, perhaps God performed a miracle and took it to Heaven, body and all, immediately after it was born, thinking that there were already too many children with no father and no money in that house. My aunt was sad for a long time, but even so she always said that it was better that way, above all for that poor creature who was now happy in Heaven. Maybe they didn't tell the truth because it would have been difficult for people to believe it. It is difficult to believe in miracles, Ana, but they exist."

Any story of Domitila's entranced her small listener, who kept thinking about the story for hours after getting up from her seat in the kitchen. But for the little girl the best story was the one about the old woman's grandmother.

They brought her grandmother from Africa to work as a slave on a sugar plantation. On arriving in the new land, they gave her the name Esperanza, and since she was young and healthy, they assigned her to the owner's house. There she served the master's wife, who was expecting her first child. The girl spent her days lamenting her fate. She missed the place from which she had been taken by force, missed her family, her native tongue.

A short time after her arrival she met a slave, a worker in the cane fields, and they fell in love. In that love Esperanza found the solace to endure all her sorrows. With him she could speak, and on embracing him the horror of her destiny hurt her less. But their brief encounters became more and more difficult to repeat, especially after her mistress gave birth to twin girls that Esperanza was expected to care for day and night. She didn't mention her feelings to the *señora* because she was certain that it would only make the situation worse. She spent her days waiting for an opportunity to run off to the slave quarters where Braulio slept. Her escapades were discovered when she became pregnant. From then on she was kept under constant vigilance. She gave birth to a girl who was snatched away from her a few days after being born and who grew up to be Domitila's mother.

Devastated by the separation from her daughter, Esperanza hated her masters with a borderless rage, with a hate that extended to everything they loved and all that belonged to them, including the twins. One unbearably hot night at bedtime, Esperanza put into each of their bottles the strychnine that they used in the house to kill the wild dogs that surrounded the farm. After feeding the girls, she mixed a generous quantity of the powder with some lemonade that she drank in one gulp. The three of them now dead, she began to fly, gripping each of the twins firmly by the hand, and she took them back to heaven, from where they had come. Now alone and free, she didn't stop until she got to Africa.

The stories fortified by Domitila's words were the most coherent that Ana ever listened to. The old woman responded to her questions in a direct manner, without preambles, and as a result became an unquestionable source of truth. Everything that Domitila said was true because she said so, but the world the old woman created was lacking in events that could prove her right.

The little girl viewed life from two angles. On one side she could see the confusing precision of her family life, and on the other the clear abstraction of the cook's stories. The union of these two perspectives became the way in which Ana saw the world, one that belonged only to her and where the events of daily life were explained in Domitila's way.

So one day, when Ernestina and her mother were commenting on the death of Matilde, Ana's maternal grandmother, which had occurred years ago, the little girl asked where the lady had flown after her death. Ana received one of those looks, in between surprised and mocking, that were frequently directed towards her, and they responded that they didn't know where she had gotten that from, that people didn't fly. The child grew quiet. Later in the kitchen, she sat next to Domitila, who was drinking coffee, and questioned her without preambles:

"Why did your grandmother fly when mine didn't?"

The old woman responded immediately, with no sign of doubt in her answer:

"Because to fly it is necessary to have suffered a great deal. This is the only way to learn how to do it, and I don't believe that anything as sad as what happened to my grandmother ever happened to Señora Matilde."

Ana got up and left the kitchen, satisfied with the answer. People could fly, but to be able to do it, certain requirements were necessary.

That Sunday, the eve of Three Kings Day, she got up without having decided what it was she wanted. Her mamá and grandmother had already asked her many times in the past few days, and they had warned her so often that she was waiting too long and that they couldn't guarantee that the Kings would be able to find what she wanted at the last minute, that they gave up insisting.

On hearing the question, the little girl had looked at them in silence. She wanted things, of course she wanted them, but the Kings wouldn't bring any of them. She would have liked to have a little brother, but she had asked for that a lot, and according to her mamá it was impossible for health reasons and according to Domitila impossible because Ana was *abicú*.* She didn't understand either of their explanations, but she did understand that she wasn't going to be satisfied. She would have liked to have more friends, but the Kings didn't bring people, and they always bought what she asked for without the need for special days or wise men. The best gift that she had ever received in her whole life had been the dolls Aunt Clemencia had

---

* abicú: A Yoruba word used for a child (a spirit, really) that makes it impossible for its mother to have more children.

made for her, and she hadn't even had to ask for them. She didn't want to ask for toys from beings for whom nothing was impossible. It would be the waste of an opportunity to get something unique.

In the middle of the morning her mamá asked her if she needed help writing the letter. Ana answered that no, she knew how to do it by herself. But at lunchtime she was still downcast, and Grandmother Teresa asked Domitila to take her to a matinée.

In spite of her great love of the movies, she paid almost no attention during the first half-hour of the film, obsessed with her request to the Kings. After exactly forty minutes, a fairy appeared on the screen. Ana dragged her little body forward and remained on the edge of her seat, neck tense, head motionless, for the rest of the movie. When the show ended, she headed straight for home, without even wanting to stop for ice cream. It was past five in the afternoon when she wrote carefully,

Dear Kings:

I would like you to bring me a magic wand.

Kisses,
Ana

Satisfied with her decision, she folded the letter carefully, placed it in an envelope, and leaned it against one of the pots of lemon balm on her bedroom windowsill, looking towards the garden to facilitate her vision from outside. What luck to have gone to the movies! With a magic wand she could make friends, she could play with them in her room and could make them disappear when they were finished playing or the adults arrived. And the best was that when she wanted them again she could get them. Perhaps it would even be capable of making her a brother.

While Ana, having finished her writing, dreamed under the big tree in the patio, her mamá read over the letter. Faced with her daughter's indecision, she had accumulated numerous toys. She had bought everything that her daughter had at some point mentioned that she would like to have, but a magic wand had never occurred to her.

That night, after a lot of looking in big stores and small toy stalls of the kind that stay open until late, she and Ernestina found a wand that had been hand-carved by an old man, owner of the little store where they found it. They placed it at Ana's feet, together with some of the more elaborate and expensive toys that they had gathered, because it seemed inconceivable to leave just that little stick with a star at the tip for the little girl.

However, when Ana saw the wand the following morning, she picked it up without noticing the other presents. It was not as she had imagined it, and she marvelled that such a simple instrument would be capable of performing miracles. Her only commentary was that the wand had her favorite colors, green and violet. She was sure that the Kings had painted it that way because they knew this.

She went to be alone in her room. Standing in the middle

of the bedroom, she shut her eyes, raised the small green stick with one hand and said in a loud voice,

"Magic wand, bring me a seven-year-old girl friend."

She waved her hand and opened her eyes. She waited. Nothing happened. She closed her eyes again, repeated the words and moved her arm with greater force. Nothing. The same thing happened five or six more times. Faced with her lack of success, she thought that perhaps she was attempting something very complicated. Perhaps it would work if she tried to make objects instead of people. She spent a long time trying to materialize dolls, dollhouses, colored pencils, books.

Several hours had passed when her mamá entered the room and found her sitting on the bed with an expression of disillusionment. Her eyes moist, she said without looking at her mother,

"This wand isn't magic; it doesn't do anything."

And she began to moan in deep sobs. Her mother hugged her.

"The wand *is* magic, Ana; it's just that the person who uses it needs to be a wizard, and you aren't."

This explanation, intended to console the little girl, devastated her. The sobs became inconsolable shrieks. She ran to the kitchen where Domitila was finishing the preparations for lunch. Crying and suffocated by her deep choking sobs, she related what had happened. The old woman gave her some water, sat her on her lap, and said to her,

"Listen, Ana, your mother is right, but up to a certain point. You're not a wizard right now, but you can learn to be one, and if you really want to be one and you try hard, I'm sure that you'll get there. It's just that there are different kinds of magic. I, for example, am a wizard in the kitchen. Let's see . . . Would you eat raw egg white?"

Ana looked at her and made a gesture of disgust.

"However, you love the merengues I make, and merengues are nothing more than raw egg white with sugar. But one has to know how to make them. Your mother has tried a few times, and hers don't come out well. Mine do, because I've practiced a lot and I know how to make them. And the little cookies: what are they before they become the little stars, people, and Christmas trees that you like so much? They are white flour, butter, sugar, eggs, chocolate. If I put these same things on the table now, and I tell you to turn them into cookies, would you know how to do it?"

Ana, eyes now dry but still red, shook her head no.

"Well, that's magic."

"But I want to make people," said the little girl.

"It's possible to get to that some day, but you have to start with simple things. I'm going to explain to you what you're going to do first. You're going to go to the patio, you're going to sit quietly underneath that big tree, and, very patiently, you're going to wait until a bird comes and lands on a branch of the tree, or on the grass, it doesn't matter. Then you're going to say, 'Now, bird, fly,' you point to it with the magic wand and you wave it with your outstretched hand: you'll see how it will obey you. Then you'll go to where there is a flower that is big but has not quite opened and you'll say to it, 'Flower, tomorrow morning when I wake up and come to see you, you will be open.' In this case you have to wait till the next day, but you'll see how the flower is going do what you tell it to. Little by little, each day you will be able to perform larger acts of magic. The most important thing is not to lose hope. When you get tired, set the wand aside, do something else, and when you've rested, start practicing again."

Calmer, Ana ate lunch. She felt a little disappointed that the wand didn't work as she had imagined it would at the beginning, but the idea that she could learn to use it excited her. She went out to the patio and, in effect, each time that a bird landed and she ordered it to fly by pointing her wand at it and waving her hand, it flew. But in spite of Domitila's warnings that she not attempt greater tasks, she could not help pointing at a frog and ordering,

"Turn into a snake."

Every time she tried something similar, she failed.

It was getting dark, and Ana kept ordering miracles. They had already called her twice to come eat and she answered,

"Just a little longer. Five minutes."

She understood Domitila's reasoning, but she wanted to do something extraordinary, something that was not normal and that she was capable of doing now. She looked at the sky, now dark, and thought that it looked as if a giant had filled his mouth with water, blown hard, and that each drop had become a star, there were so many out. Thinking about the many things that she would like to do with her magic, she raised her arm while she moved the little green stick with the rosy star on top. Suddenly, as she made a strong movement with the wand and looked towards the sky, one of the stars, large and luminous, began to fall. Ana followed it across the firmament with a look of surprise, her mouth open. She remembered that Domitila had told her that when this happened one could make a wish and it would be granted. And in the fleeting instants in which the star descended, she pleaded, with the vehemency that only a seven year-old girl can muster,

"Little star, don't fall."

And before her perplexed eyes, the star stopped its vertiginous fall, turned itself over and began to rise, and rose until it became a brilliant point fixed in the highest part of the sky.

Ana remained motionless for some instants, contemplating it. She felt a joy unknown until then, a happiness greater than going to the movies. She could only compare it to that of some dreams. It was how she had imagined she would feel if she knew that her mamá was never going to cry again or that she was never going to come home from school early to find her papá in Zuleika's room.

She had to tell Domitila about it, and she ran to the house without worrying about stepping in her footprints.

ANA AND THE SNOW

What most impressed her about the snow was the silence. Two days before Christmas, exactly two months after her arrival, daybreak found the garden white, and she found the quietness of a nature she wasn't used to disconcerting.

"I didn't hear it. I would have liked to watch it start to fall. It probably started while I was still awake, since it takes me so long to get to sleep in this vile place," she thought in that language that perturbed and frequently bothered those who listened to the elaborate rhetoric leave such a young mouth.

But had so much time really passed between going to bed and falling asleep? On two or three occasions, Diane and Mark mentioned during breakfast that howls were heard near the house during the night. She never heard them, and the time they said they had heard the wolf was when she had just gone to bed. Could she be sleeping without knowing that she was asleep? Did her sleeplessness not last as long as she thought? The idea worried her; there were too many things that had happened to her lately without her realizing.

But in Purgatory everything is possible, she thought dejectedly, and she felt her stomach tighten up and keep tightening until there was extra space inside her, a piece of herself empty.

She slowly contemplated the garden. She didn't like surprises. The ground, the barren branches of the trees, the bushes whose leaves didn't fall planted next to the fence that bordered the sidewalk, the bird feeder, now empty of birds. All covered. And so much white silence made her afraid. Even more afraid, because she woke up afraid every morning, and on feeling herself awake, prayed, her eyes still closed, that when she opened them the landscape outside her window would be different from that of the night before. If it was, her punishment would be over. She closed her eyes lethargically.

She woke up again ten minutes later. In a state of alertness, she touched her temples, but her eyelids were slow to open and face the task of living a new day, a task that seemed terrifying. What a word. She had heard it from her father's mouth a few days before leaving the house, and he could never have imagined how useful it had been in these months. She said it . . . she thought, to be exact, daily. It was terrifyingly unfortunate—and she smiled on hearing in her imagination the sound of the disproportionate phrase. She liked it. If she had been in her house, she would have brought it out during a Sunday lunch; Grandmother Teresa would have paused the fork she was raising towards her mouth, turned her face to look at her, and exclaimed,

"What a cheeky little girl this one is, if she hasn't turned into a two-bit philosopher on us."

Her house . . .

She opened her eyes and observed the leafless tree near the window next to her bed. The curly little ribbon on top of each of the branches reminded her of the meringue border on Domitila's cakes and her smile as she approached the dining room table holding the cake in both hands. Had she ever told her how much she liked the cakes she made?

"Your cakes are the best in the world, the best," and she hugged her.

Yes, she had told her; she saw the scene clearly, felt the heat from her neck on throwing her arms around it, felt the damp of the cook's large and sweaty chest against her small one.

She felt it, yes. But she tried to make out the features of her face in that moment and was unable to. She tried shutting her eyes hard, and began to see green and purple circles that widened and closed.

Why had she never told Domitila how much she liked her cakes?

She felt cold. She pulled the blanket that she had kicked down to the foot of the bed on waking up toward her, and covered herself up to her neck, holding herself with her fists held close to her body. She shivered. She smelled pancakes.

"Smell of pancakes, called to breakfast in five minutes," she whispered.

She would respond the first time she heard her name, although her first impulse on hearing it was to hide under the bed so she wouldn't have to go down to the dining room. But her goal to improve her behavior obliged her to go eat as soon as they called her. She even ate Diane's soup without talking back.

Leaning against the headboard of the bed, legs close to her chest and the blanket clutched under her chin with both hands, she made a face with her mouth while thinking of that soup, in which thick white noodles floated, when she only liked the soup that Domitila made, with angel-hair noodles, really fine and yellow. Hopefully they wouldn't make it today. It was Saturday. On Saturdays she ate breakfast and then returned to her room with the pretext of doing her homework; she had a lot due for Monday. In reality, she returned to tormenting herself without interruption.

In her own house she was slow to get up to go to school.

And to go eat. How many times they used to call her. There were afternoons when it was five. And there she was sitting under the mango tree. She would dawdle on purpose. To punish her mother for crying, her father for making her mother cry, her grandmother for not scolding her father when he made her mother cry, her aunt for being indifferent to her mother's crying. She revenged herself on the grownups by being late. Revenge for the fights in front of her, for her sadness on seeing the dark circles under her mother's eyes that appeared each time her father arrived home early in the morning.

The mango tree in the backyard. At its foot she dreamed about the day when her brother would be born, or about the moment in which, with her magic, she would make a little friend. She would make her invisible, so they could live together without being bothered by anyone. How she enjoyed staying there for hours, even though they punished her for it by not allowing her to go to the movies on Sundays. All those episodes of *The Desert Eagle* that she had missed because of the mango tree. What were those episodes about?

She still didn't understand. It didn't matter that on arriving at the Miami airport silent and with fear-filled eyes and not finding Aunt Clemencia there waiting for her, they had explained that it was for her own good, that it was necessary to save her from Communism, that she was safe now, no one would take her to Russia, she would be reunited with her parents soon, they would come to get her, and she would live with them just like before, better than before. Now they were waiting for a very nice man and woman who lived in Iowa and who would take care of her until her parents arrived from

Cuba. She was very lucky that these people had offered to take care of her. "Iowa? Iowa?" And their explanation seemed to be farther off each time. They would be here in just a moment. A very nice man and woman.

"It's for your own good, it's for your own good," repeated the older man, who pronounced "Russia" with an "r" like "*pero*," not "*perro*," which is how one says "*R*ussia." And, far from the moment, Ana paid more attention to how the man pronounced the words than to their meaning, incapable of accepting the desolation of that unforeseen reality.

The reasons the man gave bounced off the girl's ears. He talked, and she sweated. And she saw green and purple circles that on bursting became waves that moved from left to right, and between them was the house in Havana and her family, and in the middle of the man's incessant conversation, Ana tried to figure out if the scene in front of her had ever existed, if it had been hours or years since she had lived it.

On the porch, standing in front of the armchairs whose shiny wood she contemplated fixedly, waiting for her father to take the car out of the garage to take her to the airport, she saw the same people, her mother, her aunt, her grandmother, and the patio with the same birds: the swallows, the *toties*, a *tomeguín*, a *zunzún*. Ernestina's dogs, Ernestina's fastidious dogs. Only Domitila was missing from the porch, but she could see her too, because between the purple and green waves the house had no walls or divisions. Domitila sulking at the kitchen table. On seeing her father park in front of the house and her mother open the door to get in, Ana ran to the cook and kissed her on her cheek, which smelled of *Hiel de*

Vaca soap. The old woman caressed her face with both hands without moving from her chair, her father leaned on the horn impatiently, and Ana preserved the memory of that moment like a soft touch, of a softness almost impossible coming from such a rough hand. A little farther away, four blocks from the house, was the school she always went to; a little later, at mealtime, were always the daily family arguments.

And where were those "always" now?

She heard her mother's voice.

"Of course she'll be waiting for you at the airport. Just like last year. She's dying to see you, and she says she has the cloth for the dolls you're going to make together all ready. This year she's going to show you how to make them yourself."

And Ana opened her eyes in a gesture all her own of contentment, imagining herself going home, bringing in her hands a doll just like the ones Aunt Clemencia made, made by her.

"You leave on Friday. We have to be at the airport very early, because travel has gotten complicated. Now it's a mess, and there's a ton of paperwork to take care of before boarding."

She didn't even protest the long wait at the airport and the coming and going from different ticket windows. She happily put up with everything, excited about the fact that the flight was only forty-five minutes, as her mother said, and that Aunt Clemencia would be there waiting for her. She liked to go to her house.

Aunt Clemencia had died a month before Ana got to Miami, her mother told her when they met again. She told her, with great shaking sobs, that when they had planned Ana's trip her aunt was still alive and happy to take care of her until she and her father left Cuba, but things got so bad that she had died of some strange illness, something related to beef imported from England, because since Clemencia had taken a liking to England thanks to her British friend, the only meat she ate came from there. Her friend had also died in a strange way. A strange destiny, Clemencia's, living in Miami since 1947. The only one in the family; no one else had ever thought of living off the island, but she was influenced by those friends she hung around with. They were Clemencia's only problem, those friends. They should never have included Clemencia in their plans, but who could have imagined; she was in the best of health, she only suffered from arthritis and there was no threat of that killing her, not in twenty years, and the most important thing was to get Ana out of Cuba. The danger was imminent. "You can expect anything from those people."

Lies, all lies, Ana repeated to herself, mute and dry-eyed, the night she got to Miami. She repeated it like a mantra the whole way to Iowa. And it seemed such a lie to her, that her mother and father and aunt and grandmother should have invented such a macabre story, should have taken her to the airport and put her on the plane alone, so that a tall older man could wait for her in Miami and tell her that story about Russia, so that a blond woman, also tall, whom she had never seen before, whom she didn't even understand, could put her on another plane and take her to place where another tall man, younger than the man that had met her at the airport in Miami, was waiting for her, and that they should go from there to a place where everything was strange, where she didn't like what they ate, where her only comfort was to go to bed as early as possible in order to cry for the longest time possible. So unreal was everything, that one morning, two weeks after having arrived, when they woke her up to go school and it seemed impossible to her that she be able to bathe herself, dress herself, swallow the cereal with milk that they served her and face her teacher and classmates, who terrified her because they seemed absolutely foreign, she thought, with a clarity made transparent by logic, that she was in Purgatory.

She had died. This was the Purgatory that Grandmother Teresa had talked about. Not Hell, because there there was fire and they burned you, and they weren't torturing her like that. It wasn't Heaven, because in Heaven one is happy, and she was very sad. And she tried that morning, while the teacher explained some mathematics rules that she didn't understand at all, to clarify her situation, remembering everything her grandmother had told her about Purgatory.

"It's a place where one suffers for a time, until one pays for the sins for which you were sent there."

It wasn't forever, she remembered that part well, and she felt enormously comforted on remembering it. So what she had to do was obey and wait for the time to pass. She now realized that the adults were right. She was badly behaved, surely really badly behaved, what had happened was proof of that. She had never thought that she was so bad; if she had known . . . she would have paid more attention to her grandmother. But even considering her guilt, they should have told her how long she was condemned for. She didn't remember the trial. But neither did she remember having died.

"You keep climbing that tree," she heard her grandmother's voice, "You're one step away from falling and breaking your neck. There won't even be time to take you to the hospital. It'll be an instant death."

Even Domitila said it, and she rarely scolded her. But even making a detailed recount of the scoldings and warnings, she couldn't fix the moment in which she had broken her neck. In spite of everything, it calmed her to relate her exile to her disobedience, and to find a name for the place of her abandonment.

At that moment, she decided to accelerate her learning of English, and she told herself that it was the month of "November," and that she had to pay attention to the teacher. On arriving home that day, in two hours she memorized the names of the months, the days of the week, and the numbers up to 365, repeating them each time she got to the end. She wanted to speed up the time. Why it occurred to her that repeating the numbers of the days in a year would reduce her wait she never understood, not even as an adult.

Everything was white beyond the glass. Even the ledge of the window, where two boxes filled only with dirt were balanced, was now covered with snow. When she arrived, the flowerpots didn't have any flowers, but they still had plants, almost dried out. Would the grass still be green under the thick layer of white?

Leaning against the headboard of the bed and always covered up to her chin, she watched the snow fall and thought how different it was from the rain. The sound. When it fell, and even before it fell, it announced itself. The yard, the backyard of her house. How lucky that in Purgatory they didn't take away your memory. Thunderclaps, flashes of lightning, and the downpour onto the pots of lemon balm balanced on the ledge of the window of her room. The lemon balm smelled more after a rain.

She followed the trajectory of some large flakes as they fell, saw them touch the grass of the garden, break apart, and accumulate to form a thicker and thicker carpet, and she felt afraid. The silence scared her; she wasn't used to it. Nor to the snow, nor to the meals with few conversations, held in a low voice, during which she couldn't help but miss the arguments between her mother and grandmother that had so tormented her when she lived them.

The night of her arrival, two months ago, after eating a bowl of cereal in silence, put to bed in the white and mint green room, recently painted for her, she tried to understand, but only managed to cry. She had never seen signs in Cuba that they wanted to take her to any place that she didn't want to go to. Russia? Now she *was* somewhere she hadn't asked to go to, nor had wanted to go to. Maybe she could talk to the woman and her husband, or the man she thought was the husband because he had gone to wait for them at the second airport. She would do it the next morning. The next morning she had breakfast with the couple reluctantly and silently. How was she going to tell them, if she didn't know how to say it?

She continued to have no appetite, in spite of the vitamins

they prescribed for her, and the gym class they made her take at school, a disagreeable task that she accepted happily after her plan to reform, as part of her penitence.

After a month in the new house she understood more English than she appeared to. She preferred to remain silent and to shut herself in her room as soon as she came home from school to contemplate the knife she had brought with her and hung in front of her bed. A little knife for cutting cane, smaller than normal and not very sharp, that they had bought in a souvenir shop during a trip to a sugar mill in Matanzas. Her father thought it crazy to give in to the little girl's whimsical desire, that among the hundreds of available tchotchkes in the market she preferred a knife for cutting cane, even though it had a typical landscape, two palm trees in front of a mountain and a river that descended between the trees, drawn on one side.

"Who would think of buying a thing like that for a nine year-old child?"

It occurred to her mother, who would agree to anything to quiet a temper tantrum of Ana's. And Ana became so attached to the toy that she took it on their walks, even though it was necessary to buy her a bag for this purpose. There was no way to convince her not to bring the artifact with her to Miami. In Iowa she didn't bring it along with her on walks. She made them hang it on the wall, in front of her bed, and she spent long hours looking at it, imagining how, with one blow, she could cut off the heads of everyone around her. Again and again she chopped at heads that rolled on the floor bumping into each other, their hair reddened with their own blood and the blood of others. With this vision, Ana felt the nagging pain that weighed her down each hour that her eyes were open lessen. Asleep, she dreamed about the severed heads in a recurring dream that seemed to recur because it was a replica of her daily imaginings.

As a woman, Ana would talk about the period in which a large part of her energy was spent controlling her almost uncontrollable desire to take the knife down from its place on the wall and use it.

"Ana, get dressed, because we're going on a walk. It's snowing. You'll see how pretty it is," said Diane, smiling, appearing at the door to her room.

Ana got up, got dressed, and after her usual frugal breakfast, they went out.

The little girl that sat next to Diane in the car that morning was a taciturn child who had been there two months and celebrated her tenth birthday one month before with a chocolate cake that had *Happy Birthday Ana* written across the top, a little girl whose weight her adoptive mother struggled to maintain at a normal level through vitamins and an insistence that she not get up from the table without having put something in her mouth.

Ana seated her skinny little bad-tempered body next to Diane and turned her face towards the street, indifferent. She remained indifferent until, on passing by one of the houses, she saw some children making a snowman. Fat, with a round nose and a pipe in his mouth. Ana looked at it with what, for her, was an unusual attentiveness, and continued to observe it after they had passed, turning first her head and then her whole body. On encountering a second group of girls making another snowman, she asked Diane to stop the car. More than five minutes in a state of absolute attention, her face pressed against the glass of the car window. On returning home two hours later, clutching a cigar that she had begged her adoptive mother to buy, and for which they had visited four different establishments in the city, something in her expression had changed. She even seemed content. Diane glanced at her during the trip home, asking herself why she wanted the cigar.

Early the following morning, reviving a habit of getting up early that she seemed to have left in Havana, Ana got up, breakfasted on the juice, cereal, and milk that they served her, and on finishing, to the astonishment of Mark and his wife, said, with a courtesy that they had not imagined the little girl knew how to express in English,

"*May I have a cup of coffee, please?*"

They were not used to having a little girl drink coffee, but their happiness at having shared a normal meal for the first time and the school psychologist's warnings about cultural differences meant that her wish was immediately granted.

Holding the cup in both hands, she went out to the patio. She began to drink slowly, placing the cup on the stump of a tree that served as a table, and with great care and patience, began to build a snowman, spending almost all the hours of daylight engaged in the difficult task for which she possessed no experience. From the living room window, Diane and Mark observed the detail that Ana put into shaping the wide nose, and almost as the sun set she finished a pair of thick lips, between which she placed the cigar she had made them buy. Astonished, the couple watched the end of the process. Ana wrote on a piece of cardboard that she hung around the neck of the snowman: DOMITILA. She brought her lips close to the white cheeks and kissed them. She murmured something, then entered the house with a red nose and numb hands.

Contrary to all their fears, Ana didn't catch a cold during that winter's long early hours, when, seated on the tree trunk in the patio, in front of the Domitila she had built with her hands, she drank coffee and carried on conversations that only she and the old snowwoman understood. Since her arrival in October—and it was now the end of December—she hadn't spoken Spanish. She had told no one about her nightmares or her desolation. She told Domitila everything. She asked her everything: Why had they sent her to this place, why hadn't they told her, why without her knowing, why had they tricked her? She was never going to love her parents or her grandmother again. Domitila, yes, because she hadn't known either. She cried and dried her tears quickly so they wouldn't have time to freeze on her face, and her runny nose was even harder to control as soon as she started her laments.

Domitila, always with the unending cigar between her lips, because Ana brought it into the house at night and returned it in the morning ("She never smokes at night"), was her confidante, as she was in Havana. The girl began to eat regularly and to talk to Diane and Mark a little. She spent hours in front of the knife hung on the wall of her room.

One very starry night, while she walked from the patio

to the house, she remembered the magic wand that she had asked the Three Kings for years ago, and her wish that the little pink stick with a green star at the end that her mother had left under the bed for her would bring her a brother, bring her a little friend. She looked at her cold Domitila who warmed her heart every morning, and suddenly a great happiness made her breathe deeply and rapidly when something—someone?—told her that she didn't need magic wands or spells to create people, animals, even gods if she wished. She only needed her hands and wood, her hands and rocks, her hands and snow. She was already a magician. And she went into the house, convinced with the absolute certainty that only a ten-year-old girl is capable of, that she and her quiet Domitila communicated with each other.

Ana retouched her snowwoman each morning, but the intense cold of that winter helped to keep her intact. Her work was so good that the neighbors visited just to see it, and someone suggested to Diane and Mark that if Ana stayed in the city through the next school year they should sign her up for sculpture classes.

At the beginning of April, melting was imminent, and one morning, as Ana was going out with her coffee, she realized before sitting down on her tree trunk that the tilting of Domitila's head indicated that it was beginning to melt. What froze then was her heart. The sun shone, and she hated it the whole way to school. She returned anguished, and there was no way they could get her to eat. She sat in front of the sculpture, watching how, drop by drop, the eyes, the nose, the lips disappeared, how the shoulders became deformed and the arms blended into the apron. Past midnight, sleep overcame her as she sat on the tree trunk on which she rested her cup of coffee in the morning. Diane and Mark, powerless to bring her out of her sadness, watched her from the window, waited until she fell asleep, then picked her up and put her in bed.

When day dawned the following morning, April 17th, only the lower part of Domitila's skirt was left. Ana didn't go to school; she lacked the strength to stand. Around noon a call came from Miami. The girl's parents had arrived from Cuba. Diane and Mark brought her to be reunited with them. So ended for Ana the experience that had made her more independent, had hardened her to face life, had made her discover her vocation as a sculptor, and had robbed her of her childhood.

ANA AND THE LEMON BALM

Just like Aunt Clemencia's first doll, torn apart by the person she always referred to as the cruel neighbor, although they forbade her from calling him that. What did it matter that he was the son of her mother's closest friend and that both houses shared the same hedge of flower-covered *mar pacífico*, and that they went to the same school? Since the day he killed Serafín, she knew that only the worst could come from him.

As usual, no one understood her reasons. Domitila, yes, but who paid any attention to Domitila in the kitchen, except when it came to food? They didn't even pay any attention to her the only time that she intervened in a family conversation, even when it had to do with Ana and they knew that the cook was the only person the little girl talked to.

She left off washing dishes, and drying her hands slowly on her apron, she muttered in a clipped, hoarse voice like someone praying or cursing, leaning against the doorway that divided the dining room from the living room where they were gathered:

"You're crazy if you're thinking of tricking Ana and sending her to Miami alone. You must be crazy."

They looked at her without responding, not even surprised. For them, Domitila was a taciturn presence from whose hands came edible delights. Her hands were what was important, above all their cleanliness and that they be free from contagious diseases. The rest . . . Ana's attraction to her had made them all think that her mind was somewhat childlike. If not, how to explain their child's fondness for a fat black woman who was missing almost all her teeth.

Her father, her mother, Aunt Ernestina, and Grandmother Teresa, the participants in that witch's coven, as Ana baptized it years later when she found out, in that meeting to plan her destiny, exchanged a condescending look as Domitila returned to the kitchen, shaking her head in a gesture of disapproval. Teresa shrugged her shoulders before continuing with the conversation.

From any other servant, that interruption would have cost

them their place, but not Domitila. Besides her dishes, no one else was able to calm one of Ana's tantrums as quickly as the old woman. They continued to elaborate their strategy to send the little girl off ignorant of the fact that it was a trip of indefinite length.

"That's how things have to work," was the general consensus.

How could one not expect the worst from someone capable of freezing in the refrigerator of his house, seasoned with salt and lemon, the trout that he himself had raised, for which he had made his parents build a tank on the patio. How had it possibly occurred to him to get revenge on them, head held high, by opening the door of the freezer and pointing to it, ready for the frying pan, as soon as they returned from seeing Manuel, once again in the hospital for his chronic kidney problem. The hospital didn't allow visits from minors, and Tony, very attached to his bachelor uncle, made a scene the minute he was left at home.

"Manuel was the only person in the universe capable of putting up with his idiotic behavior," said Ana months later, when the uncle died.

"What a viperish tongue that girl has," stated Aunt Ernestina on hearing the comment.

"He ate it fried. He even chewed the eyes of a little fish he had named and everything."

Along with everything else that she didn't understand, Ana could never understand how the adults on both sides of the fence could consider the crime a boyish prank. Even worse, Ana overheard his mother tell hers, speaking to the rhythm of the back-and-forth of the rocking chair in which she sat each afternoon on the porch, that it was a relief not to have the thing on their patio. That's what she called Serafín. A thing. They emptied the tank the next day of the excess—the fish was too fat to be eaten by just one person—filled it with dirt, and planted it with a dozen forget-me-nots, without realizing that their having thoughtlessly chosen those flowers was Serafín's posthumous act of revenge. That's how Ana interpreted it, and Domitila sanctioned her logical deduction, sitting at the kitchen table, drinking coffee the morning after the trout's home had been used for another purpose. How could she not refuse to play with that boy?

Incredulous, dazed by the vision, she watched the dismembered doll fall, thrown from the balcony by Tony, who in an attack of fury at her refusal to be his playmate for a game of Monopoly, at which he invariably cheated, grabbed it out of her hands. He ran up the stairs and, possessed as he was—in Ana's words—grunting with rage, almost ripped off its arms and legs, sewn to the body with tight stitches by Clemencia, and threw it with such force that it landed face upward on the porch of the house in Vedado. The first thing the girl saw, now broken in two by the heartless blow against the black and white floor tiles, were the eyes, her favorites among all the dolls that Clemencia had made since they were the only black glass buttons that she had found in the box with the sign stitched on top. There had been paste eyes, wooden eyes, and eyes of different colors. She wanted black ones, and had picked out the glass eyes.

Slowly, placing great care in each gesture, she lifted the

doll off the floor, struggling to keep the chest attached to what had been the arms and legs, now just strips of torn rags that showed their scraps of stuffing. As she tried to set right the two pieces that each eye had broken into, they fell to the floor, and only the two knots of thread that had held the buttons in place were left on the doll's face.

"How much damage a cruel child can do!" stated Domitila, on picking up Ana, a crying and snot-nosed ball, off the black and white tiles of the porch and carrying her to the kitchen along with the pile of green, blue, and purple innards.

"We'll fix it; you'll see. I know how to do it."

And this broken woman who now lay on a Manhattan rooftop, who would come along to put her back together, to unite her body with the battered strips that a short while before had been human arms and legs? Who would put her eyes, knocked out in the brutal fall from the thirty-fourth floor, back in their sockets?

Domitila had died more than ten years ago, and Ana hadn't even been able to find her grave when she returned to Cuba, since they had taken her to be buried in the poorly maintained cemetery in the town of Pinar del Rio, where she had been born. By nightfall, weak from walking between dusty headstones, exhausted from pushing aside weeds to read the inscriptions, she left the flowers she had bought that morning on a grave close to the entrance to the cemetery, and dedicated it to all the old black women resting, in the most literal sense of the word, there.

Her mother, though still alive, would be incapable of confronting what were now her bloody remains. Her mother had never had the strength to console her when she had asked with words; she herself needed support and comfort too much. How was she going to do it now? Let her not see her like this! And she felt a deep pain, such as she had never in her life felt for her mother, explode inside her, imagining her pain when she found out.

Found out what? She couldn't have died; she still had time left. She was only thirty-seven. A bad death, this, if it was going to prevent her from returning to Italy to finish her work there, if it was going to interrupt her brunch with Jayne and Mel in the Mexican restaurant on this Sunday, September 8th, that was beginning to dawn. She couldn't have died on the day honoring the Virgin of the Caridad del Cobre, impossible. Without having finished the renovations on the Sixth Avenue apartment, leaving the floors unpolished, the ceiling unpainted, without having once opened or closed the bathroom door with the beautiful crystal knob that she had bought for it yesterday.

Her work. Nothing yet in the Museum of Modern Art, nor a piece in the Guggenheim. "I'm not going to live calmly," she repeated with the same rhythmic persistence on waking up every morning and before going to sleep each night, "until my work is in the big museums."

Lacking a shape to contain the pain, her suffering had no limits to its intensity. In life, her body would have responded to an upheaval of the soul like this with a headache, stomach ulcers, or high blood pressure. In life, desolation had organs where it could lodge itself. Now she only suffered.

She wanted to enter into the brokenness, pick up her guts spilled on the tiles, place each one of them inside her in the place that each had been assigned when her mother conceived her, stitch up her wounds. Arm herself, gather herself together, stand up, and give herself breath. She couldn't give herself the breath of life. Her turn had ended.

The pain stopped.

Police cars began to arrive at the door of the Deli on whose roof her remains could be found. Ambulances. One, two, three, four. Why so many, if she was so small? Why any, if they were all useless?

They approached the body, began to examine the space around it, to ask questions, to take notes. Many people gathered around her. On coming closer, most of them turned their faces away, unable to stand the sight. It didn't frighten her. She observed it calmly for the first time, with the perception of an artist, captivated by that shiny asymmetrical figure covered in a brilliant red. It was so much like one of her sculptures.

And she remembered a dream from years before.

She was in a hot, sunny country, on top of a mountain. There was a water slide like the ones in an amusement park that ran from where she was down to a beach whose sand and water she could see while she held on to the edges of the slide, ready to go down it. But the angle of the slope, an almost vertical drop, stopped her. There were people behind her waiting their turn to go down, and the only way that they could go was if she went down. She was very afraid, but in was inevitable that she go down. If her stiffness made her lean her body forward in even the slightest way, her own weight would tip her over, and she would fall down the slide headfirst. If she leant calmly back against the slide, letting herself go, everything would be all right. She closed her eyes and pushed off. The swift descent produced a calmness and a pleasure that she was never able to describe in words upon waking. When she got to the beach, the breeze was soft, the sand fine, and the seawater into which she dove, cool.

Now the calm was absolute, as absolute as the suffering before had been intense. She heard the voice of her Grandmother Teresa in her perennial naming of the seven deadly sins. She had never paid attention, but in these circumstances, and since she could hear her voice clearly, she gave herself over to an examination of her conscience. An examination of her conscience. Who would've thought.

She had not been greedy. She'd had little, and it had not been hard to share it. Waste pained her. She remembered the caramel-colored leather boots that had been too big for her, and how she had found them a new owner at the Cuban Culture Circle. They had fit Iraida well. Laziness hadn't been a defect of hers either. She had worked since she was little: what other name but work could one give to that burst of energy in her efforts to do magic, and the long hours spent dreaming awake under the mango tree in the patio or in its branches? And who was going to accuse someone who had never weighed more than ninety pounds and who was a vegetarian by nature of being gluttonous? The enormous quantity of black beans and flans she had made during her life were made with the invariable goal that the Cubans she got together with would like her more. Her lovers had been few, her love boundless, and she had been unhappy with all of them. They could condemn her for being passionate, but not for being lustful.

Pride, envy, and rage were left for the end of the recounting. More than proud, she had acted in a self-centered way on more than a few occasions. Envious she had to admit to having been, even if the Dutch Catechism said that it was, without a doubt, "the ugliest of all the sins and the most sordid." But how could she not have envied her little friends when they told her that they had been given a new brother, if she never got to have one? Or those little girls that always seemed happy, when she came to school sad, thinking about how her mother had come down to breakfast again with dark circles under her eyes? Of course she had envied those who had never known what it was like to wake up at age ten in the bed of a strange room, without knowing how you had gotten there, and to have them come tell you good morning in a language in which no sound told you anything. She envied those artists who had never been told that their art was minority art. Could that amalgam of acidity, which had hurt her more than anyone, be considered envy?

Truly truly, the only one of the cardinal sins that from the depths of the memory of what had been her human heart she would have liked to feel less if she had been able to live again was rage. How much rage had wounded her soul. In the first months of her involuntary stay in Iowa, how many heads had she wanted to sever with that little knife for cutting cane that her father had bought her at a sugar mill in Matanzas, to placate the whim of a spoiled child?

And as she became lighter and lighter, she concluded that placed in the same circumstances, she would feel and act in the same way again. She hoped that whoever was in charge of judging her would understand that she was not only finite, but also fragile and broken. And the absolute acceptance of her lack of power to have changed those situations outside of her, which were almost always the cause of her anger, brought her a deep sense of consolation.

Below, the men in white lifted the dismembered body, arms and legs almost separated from the trunk, from which spilled the mess of guts, covered it with a white sheet, and placed it on a stretcher.

The ambulances gone and the tiles of the roof returned to gray, with no trace of the shiny blood, a woman went into the Deli in search of a sandwich, and Ana from her height concluded that she must live alone and that it didn't matter to her that she was having for dinner what most New Yorkers had for lunch. She observed the window planters that rested on the floor of the balcony where she had fallen. She had never before seen the insects that she now saw eating the flowers. She should have protected the flowers from them. She should have protected . . . the insects . . . the insect . . . the flowers . . .

She was expanding without limits, the words were dissolving and her memories were beginning to fade away. A Japanese movie had said that on dying each person had the privilege of choosing one memory. Just one, in which they would have to exist for all eternity. She was sure she didn't want to remember, no, the afternoon on which she had seen her father in Zuleika's room, nor her mother's tearstained face that had confused her breakfasts as a child, nor the morning barking of Aunt Ernestina's Pekinese that had frightened the birds in the yard, nor the voice of man who had met her in Miami and who pronounced Russia with an "r" like in "pero," nor her doll, destroyed by the cruel boy, nor her rage that last night, nor the insects that inhabited the balcony where she had fallen. She didn't want to remember any of this.

She didn't have much time left, and her eternity was at stake. It would be nice to remain in the afternoon of Aunt Clemencia's first doll, or in the moment of her first miracle, when the shooting star changed its path to obey the small magician, or the day on which Domitila told her about her dead grandmother's flight to Africa, or the morning in Iowa when she had made the snowwoman to whom she could speak in Spanish and from whom she had learned that the magic was in her own hands, or in the contemplation of one of her silhouettes, those placed in the earth, those that floated, her silhouettes of flames, her goddesses in the Escaleras de Jaruco. Would anyone visit them as time passed? Would the visitors remember, on contemplating those solid Taino women, the woman that had made them? Would anyone tell them about her love of making them, about her happiness, upon finishing them, at knowing that a trace of her would always remain in Cuba? Cuba.

Ana felt herself inhabited by an unknown clarity. Light, alert, but sure that in a few instants there would be no room for memory in her new state. Her memory remained locked in what would be transferred to a cemetery in the Midwest of the United States. And she felt an enormous restfulness at the certainty that in her new home there would exist only one memory, and that it surely wouldn't be that of her burial.

It was getting dark. With the last ray of sun she would go too, and she still hadn't decided. She looked down once more. Manhattan was no longer there. It was the window of the room in which she had slept on the first night of Aunt Clemencia's visit. It was the night she had found the moon and the flowerpots, which today seemed to be even more in bloom. And with an intensity that resides only in the eternal, she was enveloped by the scent of lemon balm. And she left.

Like in Jail

How will kisses taste?
What territories will caresses
 discover?
What horizons will stand revealed at
the hour of love?

—Margarita Drago

If they hadn't locked me up I would soon have ended up bald. In the months prior to my detention, this image fixed in front of me before opening my eyes, I would wake up searching for the lock of hair that I had left on the pillow during the night, frequently enough hair for me to buy the idea of an immediate baldness.

They came during the day, but I waited for them at night. That was why I curled up next to my mother in bed, seeking a heat that I had refused with obstinate insistence since I was a small child, fleeing her excessive protection. Curled-up, not daring to ask for it, internally I begged her to caress me. She, whose caresses I rejected as excessive, whose complaints and laments tormented my childhood. Had the shame of revealing an emotion that I, at twenty-five, said and thought I did not harbor not been stronger than the fear, I would have begged that she hold me against her warm breasts, that she call me her little pigeon. Yes, I would have begged her to use the ridiculous name that I had told her not to call me so many times, and that invariably left her lips when we found ourselves at home after each trip to the hospital where she had been, when her complaints and laments had made my father fear a suicide attempt. Or maybe it wasn't even that, maybe he was the one that felt his resistance to putting up with her sickness give way, and I was thankful for the paternal decision, the silence, the temporary peace at home. When I was little, unaware that I was thankful for it, later knowing it, even though the feeling made me feel guilty.

Nerves, it's nerves, said the doctor I went to about losing my hair. Fear, I told myself. And on leaving the doctor's office I returned home thinking, and went to class thinking, and ate thinking, and slept the little I slept thinking that my only alternative was to learn to tolerate the fear. I didn't stop passing out flyers at the university, I didn't stop turning in the clandestine literature that the union assigned, I didn't stop editing the calls for strikes and protests. I wouldn't, I couldn't stop. Stronger than the fear of the certainty that they would come get me was the fear I felt at the thought of not doing what I considered my revolutionary duty. They could kill me, but in that moment of being afraid, I was alive. With a deathly fear, but alive. To give in, to stop doing what I considered my duty, would be immediate death, an inability to look at my face in the mirror. I would cease to be in the exact instant of betrayal, no matter how many years my body would be walking the streets, even with my mouth smiling. I wouldn't exist; and now, dead with fear and almost bald, I did.

They came for me by day, a morning when I was still shuddering at the shock of waking up and searching for the lock of hair on the pillow. It was summer; ready to leave for the university, I was wore a short-sleeved dress and some sandals with a wide inch-and-a-half heel. I spent seven years on that inch-and-a-half heel. I entered and left the jail in those sandals.

Apart from death, the greatest fear in my nightly and daily terrors, prior to the presence of soldiers at the door of my house, was a fear of a lack of freedom to walk the streets with their sidewalks sown with oranges in the provincial capital where I grew up, and of the heat that I would feel locked in a small cell without even a tiny barred window. I can't stand the heat.

I resisted. Beatings, verbal and physical humiliations. Weeks spent in solitary where they gave me a mattress at night and took it away at six in the morning, where I spent the day lying on an iron slab, trying not to lose the sense of days, only to realize later that it was impossible to calculate the sunrises and sunsets, that I was unable to tell what month, day, or time it was.

An eagerness to wake up alive each morning made me forget my need to walk the streets, and most of the time I felt a cold independent of the weather. An internal cold that wouldn't let up and that grew in the presence of the jailor, above all in my first months in prison and with the memory of my mother's laments and demands. I told myself then that I was a prisoner, locked up in jail, and that she couldn't follow me there.

It was a cold that lessened during the conversations with the other women in the jail and during the clandestine study groups that we held. A cold that almost disappeared when we managed to take a drink, on holidays, of the liquor that we made from the apple compote that our families brought on the visits when they were permitted to bring us something sweet along with menstrual pads and the medicines we asked for. The color and taste of the crudely fermented apple were disgusting, but after downing it, making faces, and not breathing, the feeling of lightness in the head that it gave us, and the laughter we managed to squeeze out of our tales of misfortune, were tremendous.

I was always vain. I still am; it's a quality that I recovered as soon as I was free again. On being taken prisoner, they gave me a blue uniform with pants of a thick and un-ironable cotton, with an elastic waist, and a blue shirt with a v-neck and long sleeves. The same style and color for summer and winter, in a flannel model for the cold months. The well-cared-for short hair that I came in with grew formlessly until it reached an appropriate length for me to tie it behind my head with a rubber band. Make-up didn't exist, and we only colored our lips and cheeks, relying on our inventiveness, to receive visitors. With great difficulty, we managed to keep our teeth clean and maintain a minimal personal toilette. To my own surprise, on being in solitary, I at once realized the relief and the sense of internal freedom I gained from being denied the possibility of wearing makeup. We didn't have a mirror, so the only image that we could observe of our own faces was the reflection we saw in anothers' eyes. Four in a tiny cell that (left un)satisfied our most peremptory needs. There we slept, we defecated; when we had something special to cook, we cooked it on a small stove located in the corner next to the latrine.

As soon as I was taken prisoner my hair stopped falling out. After a time, one midday, lying face up on my iron bed after having devoured the broth they gave us for lunch and after having listened to a long philosophical reflection, directed, as always, by Damiana, which consisted of being truly revolutionary, we decided to take a nap. Everything had been done calmly: the ingestion of the greasy broth, the conversation over the meal, the limitless rest we were taking. We could sleep twenty minutes, thirty, an hour. What did it matter? And I realized that among so many losses and limitations, I had something that I had been missing before coming here, always buried in projects and struggling to reach certain goals. I had time. Time. I don't know if that's a precise name for the morning after morning of those days beyond the calendar, days marked only by our talks, days that little by little created a previously unknown intimacy that I had never had with anyone, not with family, or boyfriends, or friends, in part because I had never had time to build it. What we had now was an extreme situation about which we never said anything to each other, because this absolute time that we enjoyed could be the last; we might not be alive the next morning, and a raw awareness of this had developed in us. Not all of our talks were pleasurable. We discussed our weak points, our flaws, our failures in love; we cried over husbands killed while being tortured, but as dark fell we found ourselves seated on the floor fused into a hug. That we always had, those hugs.

Of the four, Damiana was the wisest, the one with the precise advice and the accurate criticism of defects that we didn't always want to recognize, that it hurt to accept. We admired her capacity to maintain us and to maintain our hope, her certainty that she would be reunited with her exiled husband. We four weren't always together in the cell; frequently one, sometimes two, three, sometimes all four, would be in solitary. There were occasions during which the cell was left uninhabited for weeks. Between María Clara and I, there was a special communion, and when we ended up alone together, our conversations were even more intimate. Seated on the iron bed, we told each other stories that we considered too small to be shared with the others, jokes, sometimes stupid things, with the sole purpose of hearing the other's voice in that space of desolation. And we played at dreaming and made lists of the wishes we would fulfill when we were free. We dreamed about feeling love again, with a man's skin next to ours. And we would hug and caress each other, and where was the line between the licit caress and the forbidden one? In that space of distorted contours and without time, it was difficult to identify it. What is the difference between caressing an arm and sliding your hand to that place where the breast is softest and roundest? And how to avoid the hardness of the nipple from the touch, and the cold, like mint, that runs through your stomach? So it happened, and after the first time, on looking at María Clara, the reflection of myself that I saw in her eyes was different, sharper, and I liked my face without make-up and the kissed lips that I could make out in her pupils. And we loved each other with an intensity that only the circumstances can explain. We knew that the rule among the political prisoners was to remain morally irreproachable, and one of the most immoral acts was love between two women. But we were happy this way, happy, in that obligatory indifference to everything that wasn't us. However, we grew silent in front of Damiana and Julia. We hid our relationship.

They accused her one morning, during our brief daily outing to the yard. A group of comrades from the Party, confined two floors above us, approached us to notify Damiana that one of the women from that floor had confessed to having an amorous relationship with her. What could she say about this matter? Damiana looked her in the eye. It's true, she responded. It couldn't be, the rest of us thought. It was true that for a while Damiana had been less talkative, more reserved, as if she had an air of worry. When we tried to ask her about it, she responded in a low voice, with that sense of humor and wisdom that characterized her, with a song: "Who told you that I was always laughter, never tears, as if I was the Spring? I'm not so much."

An ugly episode. She suffered the reproach of women who were her sisters, those she had defended until she ended up in solitary and suffered experiences that even today are hard to talk about. They shunned her. The other woman was pardoned for having confessed. Weaker, less sure of herself and her convictions, of what it meant to be a revolutionary, she couldn't resist the pressure of the group when they suspected her love affair. They never saw each other again, Damiana told us, and she continued to love all of them. They don't understand, she said, maybe some day life will make them change.

That frightening process, because this turned things upside down for months, led me to examine my conscience and, worst of all, to feel dirty. They had treated Damiana that way for an affair carried out somewhere María Clara and I could never figure out. What opportunity did they have to be alone together? They saw each other in the dining room, in the yard, and then they returned to their respective cells. We never understood, and there Damiana's discretion was absolute. What would happen when they found out about our relationship? Besides, the others were right. Irresponsible acts like these were the cause of accusations of immorality against the movement. I stopped sleeping, stopped caressing María Clara. Not even when we were alone. I avoided sitting too close to her. And I confessed. I. And I even thought that I was saving the two of us, that she would thank me after time had passed, as much as it hurt now, that my confession purified both of us, that the sacrifice of what I considered our guilty love would make us worthy to participate in the building of that new world we both struggled for. And they judged her, and my political position was lowered in spite of having confessed.

She continued to prepare *mate* in the mornings, when we had any, and to pass it to me so I could drink when we ended up sitting side by side. But she never spoke to me again or let me see my face again in her eyes. I was released from jail some months afterward and learned that she had been freed a year later. I never saw her again.

Almost twenty years have gone by. I rebuilt my life, with a lot of effort, but I managed it. I married, my children are now adolescents, and I have never again been attracted to a woman. It was a situation of circumstance, I'm convinced. What's more, I didn't remember the episode until just a while ago when Sara, a recent friend, told me she was a lesbian and that she was in the first flush of love, as my mother would say. She wanted me to meet the girl, and the three of us have gotten together a few times to go to the movies or to have breakfast, because we live close by. That's how Sara and I met, walking through the neighborhood. I like seeing them together—they make an attractive couple. One changes with the years and with immigration. For a long time after being free, I couldn't imagine having a lesbian friend. It's not that what others do seems wrong—each person has their reasons for living the way they live—but I never felt anything in common with gay people. However, now I love being with Sara and her friend. I even dreamed about them two nights ago. I, who never remember my dreams, remember this one as if I had lived it. They were together and I was sitting next to them, the three of us very close, talking and drinking coffee. I felt so good, full of a big love, difficult to describe because it's not the love that I feel in real life. It's impossible to describe.

For a moment Sara looked at me, and I saw my face reflected in her eyes, my face without make-up, with my hair long and combed back. And it was a happiness I can't explain. It was a dream about love, not love for someone, but love. There have been so few times that I have felt that sensation of fullness, that the moment is perfect, that nothing more is needed, that I had forgotten that I was capable of feeling that way. It's difficult to explain. It was . . . it was like in jail.

❊ The Eighth Fold ❊

For Maite Díaz

Lucía raised her gaze, found Ricky's eyes fixed on her, and knew she was going to sleep with him. That's how it was. He watched her as he came forward, accompanied by Verónica. They walked the distance from the door of the classroom to the desk behind which she stood, organizing papers as class was ending, and in the few brief seconds in which they crossed the meters that separated them from her, she thought about what bad luck it was that the future husband of a student of hers should attract her so much at first sight. She didn't like those kinds of games.

Now facing Lucía, Verónica smiled, revealing her even teeth and the space between the front ones. As she had promised at the last class, she said, she'd brought Ricky so she could meet him. Her fiancé extended his hand. "Pleased to meet you," and as the professor extended hers, it seemed to her that he held onto it two or three seconds longer than was usual for an introduction, unnoticed by Verónica, who gave the professor an invitation to the wedding. She asked how the preparations were coming along, and they talked about the upcoming event.

Ricky, standing behind his fiancée, quietly watched the teacher with a stare that could have been disturbing, but when their eyes met quickly during the chat Lucía responded with equal intensity. Verónica was emphasizing how much she had wanted the professor to meet him; she had talked to him so much about her classes. He really liked music too, although he didn't play professionally like the two of them did. He sold insurance.

Lucía continued to place compositions and homework into her portfolio, zipped it closed, slung her purse over her shoulder, grabbed the portfolio with one hand, and picked up her cello in the other. As the three of them left the classroom still talking, she thought that the easiness of his walk and the shamelessness of his gaze were what she liked about the man. The movements of his body gave off a freedom that bordered on a cheekiness without vulgarity, something that promised an excellent lover, since the teacher was convinced that a certain brazenness was necessary for making love in a way that satisfied her.

Ricky meditated on the way home. He had never been attracted to short women, even less so if they were as small as that lady. She wasn't any taller than four foot eleven and weighed a hundred pounds, tops; her tits looked like lemons—he'd gotten a good look at them, and her butt cheeks were too low. He remembered her watching him without blinking. "It's her eyes," he told himself, "Too big for such a small face, but there's a strength in them that makes you look at them." Her lips slid unevenly towards the corners of her mouth when she smiled, making her whole face happy. The contrast between the expressions caught his attention. It was a serious, serious face or completely smiling. The timbre of her voice, as deep as if it had come from the throat of a woman a foot taller.

According to his inventory, the woman was a mix of odds and ends; no two parts fit together. But he had liked the little teacher. He smiled inside, and on automatically turning the corner, realized that he had arrived at the apartment he had shared with Verónica for the past two years.

Now in bed, she asked him what he thought of the professor; he hadn't said anything, him, so talkative. She was great; no one who saw her, so nice and down-to-earth, would think that they were looking at a fantastic cellist. She played in the philharmonic, and had traveled around the world giving concerts. It was lucky that she had agreed to teach at the university; as a teacher she brought such an enthusiasm to her explanations that attending her class was as much fun as going to a social get-together, even though she assigned a lot of work.

"She's the only person who has managed to make me excited about studying music. You know how undisciplined I am. In spite of earning my living for so long as a singer, I've never been interested in studying music; I thought it was a useless effort—what for? I've known how to play guitar since I was little; I told you how I learned, playing with the singers that visited my house in Barquisimeto. The first time I took a course from her out of necessity, thinking it would be easy and I could get an A. I needed to boost my grade point average. The truth was that I had to study a ton, but at the end of it, to my own surprise, I wanted to know more and I signed up for another. And then for the one that I'm finishing now. It's curious that I haven't introduced you to her before. Every so often we have coffee together. I consider her a friend."

Ricky had his eyes closed, but as Verónica finished singing her praises, he asked if she was married and how old she was. And why had she dedicated herself to such a big instrument? It weighed more than she did. Verónica smiled.

"She's divorced, she has two teenage kids, a girl and a boy, and more or less our age, around forty, maybe a little younger, I don't know. You know that at this university the teachers are the same age as the majority of the students. That's how New York is."

On the way to her apartment, Lucía remembered Ricky's look. Something lit up inside of her, and she was amused by the unexpectedness of this inner turmoil.

In the following days, too many occupations demanded her time and attention for her to entertain thoughts of that encounter. She didn't think about him again.

The next Tuesday, before class began, Verónica came up to her and invited her to a party that Saturday. It was going to be just a close group of friends. There was going to be a dinner and then she and some other artist friends would play the guitar and sing. Maybe the teacher could get into it and bring her cello. It was kind of an improvised pre-wedding celebration, a last-minute idea of Ricky's, and he himself had thought of including Lucía.

She thanked her for the invitation and explained that she would try to attend; she didn't know if she would be able to, she had a prior commitment. She would try to cancel it; she knew how important everything related to the wedding was for Verónica.

There was no prior commitment. Now, a week after the effusive introduction, she remembered the incident as inoffensive foolishness, and didn't want to expose herself to a similar situation. It was better to avoid it.

However, when six o'clock on Saturday rolled around, she filled the tub with warm water on top of hot, just how she liked it. She took a long bath, took the red dress with the round neckline that she hadn't worn for a while out of her closet, sprayed herself with *First*, her favorite perfume, and at eight o'clock was ringing the bell of the intercom of the apartment in Queens where Verónica and Ricky lived. While she waited, she told herself that maybe the episode had been created by her imagination, and that she didn't care a bit about the man.

He himself opened the door, smiling. He held a glass of wine in his right hand. He extended the left with the palm up, soliciting Lucía's, who placed hers in it softly. He squeezed it, and without letting go complemented her on her dress. They walked toward the living room, where some twenty people were talking animatedly. Their attraction the other day hadn't been a figment of her imagination, the teacher thought. There was no way out of it.

She ate a few bites without appetite during dinner. After dessert, over wine, beer, and jokes, Verónica sat down on the sofa in the living room and began to sing old and new songs, accompanying herself on the guitar. They turned off the overhead lights and turned on the small table lamps, which had colored bulbs. In the dark, Lucía settled herself on a cushion on the floor, leaning against the sofa. Verónica asked her why she hadn't brought the cello.

"It weighs too much," she answered.

The group sang the familiar melodies together, clapping to the rhythm and moving their bodies to the beat. *Mi mamá me dijo a mi que cantara y que bailara, pero que no me metiera, en camisa de once varas.* Ricky and Lucía did not. They only paid attention to mutual glances, constant and hidden.

Lucía stood up, restless and dizzy. She couldn't stand to spend another minute sitting down. She walked from the living room to the dining room and, with nowhere else to go except the bedroom, where she was not going to go, went into the bathroom. As she closed the door behind her she felt a light tap. She half-opened it, and without giving her time to ask what was going on, Ricky pushed in and, once inside, closed it. Lucía leant back against the closed door, somewhere between surprised and scared. Facing her, Verónica's fiancé, with a self-possession difficult to understand in that situation, slowly placed his outstretched arms on either side of her head, pressing the palms of his hands against the door, and bent down until his eyes and mouth were level with hers. They looked at each other with all the force they had been unable to display in public. The surprise and shock left Lucía and her gaze became soft, almost pleading. He slowly came closer and kissed her, first on the neck and then on the mouth. She responded without reserve, without control. It was a frenetic meeting. Arms and legs interlaced, he moved to lower the neck of her dress and she to unbutton his shirt. In the small space, they each struggled to take the initiative in the caresses until he embraced her vehemently, immobilizing her arms at her sides, and bending his knees, slid down to the floor without letting go of her, held tight to her, kissing her over the dress that was slowly wrinkling with the pressure of his lips and teeth. Kneeling on the floor, he raised her dress and lowered her panties. Lucía let him do it. Holding her by her hips, naked from the waist down, he brought her to his mouth. As she felt his tongue and teeth playing with her body, her legs gave way; she could no longer stand. Her knees began to fold until she was sitting on Ricky's face. Reluctant to abandon his task, but needing to breathe, imprisoned between the teacher's thighs, he struggled to keep his mouth at the place of desire and at the same time to raise her body, holding it beneath her hips, as if lifting weights, to keep it at least an inch from his nose.

There was a loud knock at the door. Lucía returned her panties to the position they had been in when she entered the bathroom, straightened her skirt, cleaned her face. The dizziness passed and she recovered her strength, all in a second. She looked at Ricky with terror. By the insistency of the knocking, both of them thought that it might not be the first time that the person had knocked, and that they hadn't heard. Outside Verónica called. Placing his face next to hers, Ricky whispered to Lucía that she should say she was helping him. Drunk, vomiting. He washed his face, raised the toilet seat, flushed to indicate he had already vomited, bent his head and began to feign enormous heaves.

Lucía opened the door. In front of her, Verónica and two guests watched Ricky's convulsions with frightened eyes, as he moved the upper part of his body back and forth, moving his head to-and-fro until it almost went into the toilet bowl. Very upset, Lucía explained that she had found him this way when she got to the bathroom and that he hadn't wanted to bother anyone. That was why the door had been shut, even when she had insisted that they should call someone to help. Ricky was almost howling, so strong were the sounds coming from his throat, and Lucía's eyes were huge, apparently from desperation, faced with her friend's sudden discomfort. They raised a fuss of such proportions that, if any doubt remained about what had taken place in the bathroom, no one had the nerve to ask, even Verónica.

Lucía returned to her apartment exhausted and slept for eight hours straight, unusual for her.

From that night on, the first time three days before the splendid wedding, which was attended by more than a hundred and fifty people, among them the music professor, in intervals of never less than a week and never more than a month, Ricky and Lucía met regularly to spend four or five hours together of contained release, of intense continual pleasure, while they listened to a variety of music, always chosen by Lucía. And so on for nine months.

He called her during Verónica's artistic tours, since she traveled frequently. They would meet in Ricky's apartment in the afternoon, although there was an occasional early evening meeting. Lucía didn't stay past ten. She liked to go to bed and get up early. She would arrive with a CD or a cassette, just one that they would listen to for hours and that could have anything on it from the latest pop hits to old folk songs, or contemporary music in English, or music from the sixties and seventies. Also classical. She became so absorbed and delirious while kissing to the chords of the old bolero *Llanto de la luna* or Chopin's *Nocturne No.1* that Ricky, when that period of his life was over, could never separate those melodies from a passionate nostalgia for the teacher.

Only after their ritual bath together, where they let go of the dampness and smells acquired in hours of embraces, would Lucía open the wine that she had put in the refrigerator to chill, and they would drink slowly until they finished the bottle. She wouldn't drink while she made love; she said she preferred to concentrate on one thing at a time. Before leaving, she would carefully place the empty bottle, the cork, and any other revealing trace of their encounters in a leather bag in which she carried the music and the wine. And she would leave until the next time that he called her.

One of those afternoons, when they had been seeing each other for three or four months, at the beginning of a session of lovemaking, he commented that the wonderful thing about his relationship with her was how easy everything was, how open. There was no need to lie, to say that he was single or to swear that his wife didn't understand him. None of the other lies invented for the other women with whom he had had affairs were necessary with Lucía. She was almost perfect: good in bed—where had she learned all that?—and at the same time educated, sensitive. Your only defect is that your tits are so small, he said, laughing. She smiled without answering, and settled herself over him. Concentrating with her usual dedication on her amorous task, she savored each in and out of her lover's body, and willingly offered hers for the other's delight.

One Thursday morning, Lucía was drinking coffee in bed with her eyes still closed when the phone rang. Verónica was leaving the next day on a trip. He wanted to see her that same Friday in the evening; he missed her, but since he knew she preferred afternoons, they could wait until Saturday and have all the time they wanted. It had been a month since they had seen each other.

"Ricky," Lucía answered, "we're not going to see each other any more like we have been these past few months. It's over; I've been waiting for you to call to tell you. I'm going out with a man with whom I want to establish a serious relationship, and we're working on it. He also wants it. He's single, there are no complications, he also has teenage children, and we're trying to make things work. He's a musician like me; we share a lot of interests, we have similar needs. I'll introduce you to him."

Silence for some moments.

"I don't know how you can be telling me all this so calmly. Do you know how many months you and I have been seeing each other? A long time, and now, out of nowhere, you come out with that you don't want to see me anymore because you're seeing someone you want a serious relationship with."

"I don't want to think that you're jealous, Ricky. I don't even want to think it, because it's ridiculous. And look, if I don't go bathe now I'll get to the conservatory late. I have an early rehearsal and it takes me more than an hour to get ready. If you want, we can talk another time, but I really find this reaction absurd. This has always been a very clear relationship, without any commitment on either end. Bye, and take care."

When she got back from the conservatory she found a message from Ricky on the answering machine. He would be waiting for her on Saturday at the apartment. Verónica wouldn't be leaving the city again for another two months; they couldn't waste this opportunity. Lucía erased the message after listening to it, and went to greet her son, who was doing his homework.

Ricky called again the following morning. He didn't see any connection between her new commitment and what they shared. He also had a partner. She knew that better than anyone.

"I prefer to do things this way, and I respect your way."

He insisted on seeing her, she again gave her reasons for not doing it, and again had to hang up because she couldn't be on the phone any longer.

On Tuesday of the next week, as class ended, Lucía found herself standing behind the desk, organizing compositions and homeworks and placing them in her portfolio to go home, when Ricky entered the classroom. He had to talk to her personally, to see her face, that's why he had come. He couldn't accept that they weren't going to see each other any more.

Lucía continued to organize papers while they talked.

"I'm monogamous," she said in a calm voice. "I've never

been with two people at once. If I'm seriously with someone, I put all my energy into that relationship. I think that's the only way to give it a chance."

"And how do you square that with the fact that you've been going out with me, a married man, all these months?"

"Your marriage is your business, and you have the right to manage it as you see fit. I never interfered in your relationship with Verónica, never called you; not once did I call you to go out. We always saw each other when you wanted to or when you could, and remember my meticulousness to not leave traces of our encounters in your house. Do you think that was by chance? It was not. It was out of respect for the feelings of your wife. We were sexually attracted to each other, that was all. Apparently, you had no conflict between your attraction to me and your love for Verónica."

"And all that music, that *Llanto de luna*, those nocturnes of Chopin's, all that meant nothing to you?"

"Of course it meant something; we humans are animals of symbols and anything we make we're going to make in accordance with our condition, even licking ourselves."

"So the only thing that interested you in our relationship was the sex?"

Lucía stopped working, looked at him and answered:

"If you prefer to put it that way, I'll accept it."

"A whore is what you are, girl. A whore," Ricky almost shouted. "That's what I think. And listen to me, wherever I end up I'm going to say so every time someone mentions your name."

Lucía, already standing, raised herself up at that moment

so that she was almost five feet tall, looked him in the eye, and said, her voice as deep as ever but spacing out her words and placing a resonance on them that Ricky had never heard before:

"*Whatever you think or say can go through the eighth fold of my ass.*"

Ricky opened his eyes and his mouth at the same time. He looked at her astonished, waiting for something more, waiting for a corroboration that the sentence had come out of Lucía's mouth, asking himself if he had really heard what he thought he had heard. But she continued to organize the papers that were left on the desk without looking at him, stuck them in the portfolio, zipped it shut, and left the classroom carrying her cello.

He walked behind her, headed slowly towards the parking lot, looked for his car, went to pick Verónica up at the airport, and never said anything to anyone.

✺ Sunday at the Same Time

She separated the cartilage from the bone with a brusqueness unusual for her, and chewed. She chewed listening intently to the rhythm of her jaws and the clash of her teeth with each bite. Cartilage. She didn't remember having eaten it before. It was getting late. It's almost night, she told herself, as she looked out the window in front of her.

She imagined the sun that was setting on the other side of the buildings interposed between her view and the horizon. Night is falling, she repeated to herself. It always does at this early hour in February.

She chewed.

"What will happen . . . ?"

The memory of the phrase came to her without warning, and the resonance of her voice from then was as clear as the sound of her jaws that were now crushing the tip of the bone.

It was early, early for it to be getting dark and to be eating. She didn't eat dinner at four-thirty in the afternoon; she never ate dinner at four-thirty in the afternoon. Today she did. She shrugged her shoulders. What did it matter; today she was eating dinner at four-thirty. It wasn't that she never ate dinner early; it was that she almost never did. That's what she should say from now on. I almost never eat dinner early. She chewed.

"What will happen when it's Sunday . . . ?"

She separated a wing from the chicken and bit into it inattentively, the movement of her jaws now more measured.

From the clothesline attached to the fire balcony, her neighbor across the way was taking down the jeans she had hung out at dawn. Her neighbor liked to hang things out on the fire balcony. Well, she must like it; she did it every week. It wasn't that she liked it; it was that, if she didn't do it there, where was she going to do it? Why didn't she dry the pants in the dryer? Surely so they wouldn't shrink around her husband's belly. Fire balcony. You don't say it like that. What's a fire balcony? No one says that. Fire escape, but since her neighbor . . . she needed her name, she didn't at all like thinking of her as her neighbor across the way. Fire escape sounded better.

She almost couldn't make out the sidewalk in front.

"What will happen when it's Sunday at nightfall . . . ?"

The sound of the cartilage between her molars, now the cartilage from the second thigh that she tore with her hands from the rest of the chicken.

Her neighbor went in with the jeans folded over her arm. Plump as she is, she makes an effort not to hurt herself when climbing in through the window of the bedroom where she sleeps, first one leg, then the other. Yes, she sleeps there, although she's never seen her in bed because she sees the bed during the day, only during the day. It's curious how careful she is about lowering the curtain when she turns on the lights in the apartment when the sun sets. Only when the sun sets. If the sky clouds over during the day, no, even if it's dark in the room. The modesty and the precaution she took so that they wouldn't see the bed was curious, since she didn't mind if they saw her cry. She had cried that morning on that balcony of the fire escape. Leaning against the railing, she had cried a lot. Maybe she was so burdened with sadness that it didn't matter who saw her; who knows if subconsciously she cried there so they would see her and someone would know about her pain. It seemed crazy to feel bad and to go out to a fire escape balcony to cry in the hope that someone would console you, but you never know. If not, look at her neighbor. Here she was, in front of the window, and she saw her and felt really bad about her sobs. But the neighbor never knew.

Tears, tears for a bandit. Who would have told her when she saw that film so many years ago that it was by Saura? A little boy told her once that *Tears for a Bandit* was a movie to see on a Friday. "My eyes have never cried like they did that afternoon when I said goodbye to you." It wasn't in the afternoon; it was in the morning, and she didn't cry. In her seat in the airplane, she closed her eyes, trying not to think. Trying not to feel, not to feel how she felt. It's true that the heart hurts and shrivels up like the sad songs, the *boleros* and *rancheras*, say. "What a bunch of hogwash," she said out loud, "How ridiculous I become when I'm feeling sentimental. And why not? The truth is that I left with my heart shrunken and painful. Destroyed. And sitting here talking to the table, with my mouth full of chicken cartilage, I can think and say whatever

I want."

Sitting on the airplane, she tried to feel only the pain in her head that prevented her from raising, lowering, or turning it to either side. To close her eyes and think about the pain in her head. Any pain in her body was palliative for the other. She had to think about the pain in her head. And truly, it really hurt during the twelve hours it took her to get home.

"And what's going to happen when it's Sunday at nightfall and you're not here?"

The last Sunday, sitting on the bed. It wasn't a bed, just a thin mattress on the floor. Here in New York one was specific: a mattress two, four, eight inches wide. There, mattresses two or four inches wide were mats. Sitting on the mat, where they had spent the day, they watched the beginning of the sunset through the spaces in the blinds of the Miami window. Years ago, quite a few, when they began to make houses with those blinds, they called them Miami windows. It never occurred to her to ask what they called them now; she never needed to mention the name. Now she needed to define every kind of window; she needed to because she wanted to write it, and she could only use the word Miami to refer to those windows. Writing, making something with words. You can't make skin with words. As perfect as the description of a kiss might be, you can't create the warmth of lips with words. No metaphor is a substitute for a presence or a figure.

"I don't want to think about it."

She smiled automatically at the answer to her question. What would happen when she couldn't stretch out her arms and reach that waist, when hers was no longer within reach of the arms that embraced her now?

"Remember to pack the coat you left here last time. You always leave things: shoes, a bra, earrings. But you're going. Why don't you let the things go and stay yourself?"

Her neighbor across the way placed the recently washed jeans on the bed. It was already almost dark. She turned on the light in the room, lowered the curtain. What a odd habit, to not let anyone see what she was doing in the bedroom after it got dark.

In a final bite, she crushed the cartilage accumulated in her mouth and swallowed. Something rough brushed her trachea as it passed, and she thought she had swallowed a bone. A bone? It must have been a piece of bone; if she had swallowed a whole bone she wouldn't be able to breathe. I swallowed a bone, something sufficiently hard to have difficulty passing through the throat, the larynx, the trachea; what the Hell does it matter if it was a bone or a piece, and what the exact name is of the body part it passed through? It hurts and that's all. It's as if the screw in the brain that adjusts language had come loose, and now it's stuck there. She cleared her throat, trying to spit it out, but it was already too far down. She drank some water and felt it slowly slide down towards her stomach.

She contemplated the few remains of the dismembered chicken. Slowly, she placed the knife and fork she hadn't used on the plate, placed the clean napkin over the knife and fork, grabbed the empty glass in one hand, and walked toward the kitchen. She washed the plate, the knife, the fork, the glass.

She washed, watching the water as it fell from the open faucet. She had washed the knife and fork needlessly; she hadn't even used them, she thought as she turned off the water.

"That's what happens. You eat a whole chicken in a flash, cartilage and all, and you even swallow a bone without realizing it."

What must she be doing right now? It's the same time in Havana, even though it's still light. When it changes here it changes there, and when it changes there it changes here.

"What bullshit."

Blue Like Bluing

*As one goes through life
one learns that if you don't paddle
your own canoe you don't move.
Katherine Hepburn*

—Para Sonnia Moro Parrado

I dreamed about him. About him . . . And the misty image from the unexpected dream made her open her mouth, which filled with the water falling from the shower. She spit. Why? He hasn't been present in a single one of my thoughts for more than twenty years. "Is he even still alive? What must he be like now?" She tried in vain to remember the face that the dream hadn't shown her. "What was he like then?" His mustache, she remembered his mustache. Or did she think that she remembered his mustache? She wasn't sure even of this. She didn't believe in irrelevant dreams. Why had she dreamed about him after all this time?

Even having learned to accept her internal contradictions, she was disconcerted by this return to the memory of an episode over which she thought she had triumphed, removing it from her memory. The story was part of another life, the life of that novel-reading girl, as her aunt called her, and that movie watcher, she added later, who lived with her feet on the streets of Havana and her head in Hollywood. The one who dressed like the models she saw in *Seventeen* magazine, brought to life by Nena, the dressmaker on the third floor of Villegas between Teniente Rey and Amarguras, with cloth purchased on Muralla Street. The girl who didn't doubt—because Ingrid Bergman said it in *Casablanca* and Bette Davis in *Now, Voyager* and Vivian Leigh in *Gone with the Wind* and Susan Hayward most convincingly in *My Foolish Heart*—because that was her favorite—that she wouldn't be complete until she found THE LOVE OF HER LIFE . . . and lost him. Because that *love that one only feels once* has to be impossible. That message was repeated to her from the screen every Sunday, and on weekdays from the living room of her house. None of those interesting actresses passed through life without having suffered from heartbreak. How her mother liked that adjective. Ingrid Bergman wasn't pretty, but she was *very interesting*. Where would she have gotten the idea that Ingrid Bergman wasn't pretty? "How," Carmina asked herself in that morning soliloquy in the shower, as she spit out the water that fell into her mouth, "could I have avoided my destiny as a tropical Lolita, if those daily social gatherings presided over by my mother distilled into my ears a sentimental education whose most persistent rule suggested in an oblique, insidious, and at the same time more attractive way that a woman's life held no attraction without a forbidden love?" The official message about a woman's virtue that same mother directed at her—like that of those friends of her mother, that of her aunts and the rest of her relatives, in addition to her father's prohibitions—were weak messengers that died before reaching her conscience, beaten by the afternoon chatter that didn't take into account the girl's alert ear when praising the model of life proposed by Hollywood. After Bette Davis and Susan Hayward came Kim Novak in *Something to Remember* and Jennifer Jones in *The Indiscretion of an American Wife*. When *The Lovers* changed the rules of the game, and Jeanne Moreau, after just one, but one long and passionate night of love, abandoned her husband and daughter to run off with her lover, there was an outcry among those at the gathering. One could understand going to bed with Jean Louis Tritignant, because look how he was, not a hair on his head out of place. Who would have been able to resist him? But goodness, knowing how to cheat and keep quiet about it is elementary, stated Clara Betancourt. In six months—what am I saying?—in three months, the situation with her second husband is going to be the same, exactly the same disinterest in what she has to say, because all men are the same, and the guy will be beating her left and right just like the other one. And the boredom that overtakes her will be worse, because before she at least had the hope that changing would make things different. And that's without counting what happens if he wants her to have his child, which wouldn't be the first case I've seen. And what's the unhappy girl going to do then, leave with another one? That's what I call wrongheaded. Those women have a tragic end. *Anna Karenina* should be obligatory reading for every woman before turning eighteen. The truth is that novel is brilliant for understanding that there are lines that shouldn't be crossed. And that Caesar's wife not only has to be honorable, she has to seem so. Let me correct myself; more than being it, she has to look it.

Knowing how to cheat and keep quiet about it was the second rule from that instruction manual. And the third was that a woman gets what she wants by being good. A woman never acts intelligent with her husband, and she only contradicts him in private, in the intimacy of the bedroom, never in the living room or in front of people, because a man has to look good in public. The fourth rule, no less important than the rest, said that to keep a husband one had to be a whore in bed. How many years passed before Carmina discovered that the lives of those Hollywood stars little resembled those of the characters that her mother, her mother's friends, and she herself confused them with.

The lucubration flowed without control until she was abruptly interrupted by the memory of a song: *How far away that first date seems / when we were first brought together*, she hummed, slowly spitting out the water. And in a shiver unrelated to the temperature of the bath, without her wanting to, without intending to, there came back to her the obliviousness to everything else, even to herself, that had come over her at fifteen, during those meetings at La Copa on Fifth Avenue those Saturdays at three in the afternoon. And she smiled, immersed in an undesired blessedness. The cadence of Fredy's deep voice washing over her from the radio of his car, which at that time was called a *motorcar*, on the way to the hotel, which at that time was called an *inn*.

She rubbed her hair distractedly, with both hands, and continued rubbing for several minutes until no trace of shampoo remained. As she dried herself, she pondered the evasive dream, written on the body, bringing with it poignancy, but reluctant to be told. What was the next verse of the *bolero*? *It seems like a violet now wilted / in the book of memories of yesterday.* She could only remember it up to there, as much as she tried to keep going. The verse came back to her, transformed into more than music and words. It was an almost painful ambivalence that tightened her chest and made her breathe deeply. With a sigh, it came over her all at once, the emotion of before, anticipating the amorous encounter, and the repugnance that this softening at the memory provoked in her in the present. The car entering the motel, she with her head down, slumped down in the seat so as not to be seen. He ordered; she obeyed, to prevent one of the employees from recognizing the school principal with one of his students.

In the moment that she identified what she had lived as a great romance as abuse, lacking the power to change the past, she decided never to mention that phase of her existence. And she had never mentioned it to her friends or to her husbands or to her lovers, much less to her daughters. Not even to her therapist. And she had wanted so much to erase those two years from her memory that she had managed to do so. Well, as far as erasing went, apparently not; but she had locked them in some corner of her memory.

How far away that first date seems came back as soon as the word "yesterday" finished, the piece of the song now a recurring phrase. And with each repetition she felt increasingly that she was floating on the surface of a lake whose frozen waters were thawed by the song, and it was melting so that she could see at the bottom, intact, the story she hadn't thought about for decades. She repeated one more time . . . *In the book of memories of yesterday.* What a fucking pain! And she put on her bathrobe to go make coffee.

Leaning against the kitchen table, she stirred sugar into the full cup. Into the final rinse of a load of white clothes, her mother used to put a small pill of bluing, wrapped in a round piece of cloth tied around the pill with a string. It looked like a little woman with a wide dress. The bluing doll, she called it. She would submerge it in the water for just a few seconds, mixing it with her hand, but those instants were enough to turn it blue, and to keep the clothes immaculate until the shabby cloth was almost transparent.

Memories are blue like bluing, she thought. What's lived dyes the memory in a permanent way, even if we think that if it hurts to remember it we can erase it by refusing to mention it, and by burying it under other experiences. Memories come back, as soon as something happens to activate them. What had activated this one, and how could she displace it forever? Engrossed, she finished dressing.

On the way to the subway, she went over the previous day, searching for connectors that would bring her to the origin of the dream. A useless effort. Something curious had happened, but it was completely separate from her preoccupation.

However, it was so curious that it made her string together one of those frequent involuntary lucubrations that on some occasions entertained her and on others tortured her. Before falling asleep, she had spent quite a while forming in her head the same kind of rhyming sentences with which she was now digressing about her dream, and her past.

In life there are Miracles and there are little miracles, she told herself. The Miracles are easy to identify: inexplicable events that save your life, or get you a job, or find you somewhere to live at the moment when you don't have a place, or make you meet a person destined to be important to you. However, there are coincidences, trivial in appearance, whose hidden meaning we only understand when we relate them to a past event. She called them little miracles, and those, if you don't pay attention, pass by unnoticed.

Yesterday morning, Thursday, she had decided take the stairs down the five flights from her apartment to the street. Nothing extraordinary, she did it often as exercise. On returning from the publishing house, she took the elevator, usual for her on coming home tired, and then something exceptional happened. On entering the house, she immediately went to the kitchen and without needing to, grabbed the basket in which she kept the recycling and set out for the basement. She returned it to its place; she never did this at night, always by day, and not on just any day, only one when she didn't go to work. There were nights when it was full, not half-empty like it was now, and she would put off the task. "Why the rush today?" But an uncontrollable impulse made her grab it again, open the door, call the elevator, and go down to the basement.

She automatically began to climb the stairs, not normal for how tired she was. It wasn't an act of will; her feet led her. She was almost at the fourth floor when she ran into a man going down. She said good evening in Spanish, and when she continued to go up, he stopped her.

"Excuse me, my name is Darío. I've lived in 4B for two weeks. This morning when I left for work I found something in the stairwell that I think is yours."

He unbuttoned the two top buttons of his coat, and from the breast pocket of his shirt, a flannel shirt with blue and grey checks, took out a small brilliant object. It was the little silver hand with the closed fist that she had bought in Paraguay the year before.

"My good luck *figa*. How did you know it was mine?"

"On Monday you were in the elevator when I got in, and the *figa* caught my attention because I have one just like it."

And opening his shirt, he showed her his, almost the same size, hung on a silver chain around his neck. They spoke for some minutes about the coincidence.

"Why not call it synchronicity? It's surprising that I found it, that I knew it was yours."

"I must have lost it this morning."

And she remarked on how extraordinary it was that she should have decided to go down to the basement at that hour. She thanked him effusively, and put herself at his disposition, should he need anything. She was in 5A.

"We could grab a coffee some day," he said.

"Sure."

She went to bed pondering what that meant. Too casual

for it to be just that. The man, younger than she was, had seemed nice. She would have a coffee with him if the occasion presented itself. Before closing her eyes, she thought that his eyes reminded her of someone's. Maybe no one's; she had an overly active tendency to put features together. Sometimes it was difficult for her to tell one face from another, one with two eyes, nose, and a mouth like always. What silly things I think of before falling asleep. And then she dreamt about her old lover.

On the subway, she got a seat at the West Fourth Street stop, tremendous luck. She read the ad in front of her: "Seventy-seven percent of the leaders against abortion are men. One hundred percent will never be pregnant."

Abortions had never been a problem in Cuba, not now and not before, even before they were officially legal. Many American women had come to Cuba to have them.

It was February, but it was hot that day. She remembered that experience like one remembers some dreams, the image cloudy but the content clear. If he had rejected the pregnancy outright, it would have been easier for her to understand. A son of a bitch, she knew it now. But no. If you want to have it, it would be the greatest happiness that anyone could give me. If you don't want to, we'll find a way. Could his flexibility have been due to the certainty that I wouldn't be brave enough to drop this bomb on my mother's afternoon get-togethers, to admit that I didn't even have the finesse to hide the evidence after playing around? Why had he never had children before? Was his wife unable to? They had one later, as soon as they left Cuba, I heard. And if I had wanted to have it? Would he have talked to his wife? Would the child—girl or boy—and I live in a house rented by him, in some discreet, sufficiently out of the way neighborhood? Would the neighbors gossip that that's where the lover and the daughter of the director of the well-known school live? Would my condition as second wife, as first concubine, because who knows how many there would have been in the future, have had a destiny similar to that of Lisette, the blonde neighbor with the large mouth who visited the senator from six to ten at night, when he assured his wife he was stuck in government meetings? Would I have a husband who never slept a full night at home, and who on New Year's Eve needed dinner ready at six so he could go eat again with his official family at nine? She would have liked to ask him what his solutions would have been if she had said yes, she would have the child. Or would he have said then that in reality it wasn't possible, that he wanted it very much, but that it wasn't a good time, that we should wait? She always wanted to ask him things; she never did, because besides being her lover, and in spite of being THE LOVE OF HER LIFE, he was the teacher, the principal. He looked for a doctor. The best, he assured her. He took her in his car and stayed by her side during the abortion. Finished, they said goodbye. She promised to call him the next morning, Sunday, early. They didn't see each other on Sundays; there was the large family lunch in the house on the hill above the school with his wife, her father, her mother, her brother, and an unmarried sister. By what moral values was she governed, did they govern her? She was the first one to die, they told her. There on the island, did teachers still fall in love with their students, without their conduct having any consequences for them, or had things changed? She would find out on her next trip.

She got up late and sad, and didn't phone for fear that his wife would answer, and because of a dull resentment that she couldn't then identify. She felt fine physically, but she needed him by her side. During breakfast, someone knocked on the door. Her father opened it and told her that Rubén Carretero was there, to give her a book that she needed to read for class on Monday. She couldn't believe that he was there, that he had risked suspicion. He looked at her questioningly, from the other side of door. Nervous, from inside she smiled and took the book that she of course didn't need, but which she spent the rest of the day reading. He apologized for not having enough time to step inside, and left.

The five minutes that had passed between the three knocks on the door, which she heard as she was raising the cup of *café con leche* to her mouth, and when she watched him disappear down the stair after crossing the first landing, exhausted her until eleven at night, when she went to bed ready to fall asleep quickly so she could get up early on Monday. She spent Sunday mentally repeating each word, each movement that had passed between them during the brief encounter, remembering the exchange of glances at the door, reading and rereading the poems in the anthology he had left her, the line that said, *The happy gentleman who loves you without seeing you* resonating more strongly in her chest than the other about . . . *The vague dragonfly of a vague illusion.*

She magnified his gesture of having gone to see her, the risk he had run, having left his house on the morning of the sacred day to make sure that she was alright. On Monday, when he came up to her, on the bench under the *casia* tree, she took the book out of her school bag to return it to him.

"It's yours; I brought it for you as a gift."

While Carmina returned the book to her school bag, he told her, and it was one of the few things he ever told her, that if one day he had a son he would name him Darío.

"Why not Rubén?"

"I prefer Darío."

She had forgotten the existence of that little book, which she had left in Cuba, and his desire to give his son that name. She had no sons, but she had not wanted to name either of her daughters Daría. The episode of the abortion came a year and a half into their relationship, when she had already decided to end it, but his conduct moved her, and she put off the definitive separation another six months.

How painful this salvage operation, this stirring up of the memory to put in order some memories that besieged her and at the same time seemed so far away. She nodded off for a few minutes. When she opened her eyes, she was at the Thirty-Fourth Street stop.

She got to the new school at the beginning of October, when the semester had already started. They didn't object to her late registration because she had just moved to the neighborhood and had excellent grades. On the first day of class she was shown into the office of the principal, an extremely tall man with straight hair, dark almond-shaped eyes and thick lips that seemed to her, from the first time she kissed them, lightly rough. Next to him was his wife, a little shorter than he was, but still tall, not fat but comfortably round, as her mother would have said, with close-set eyes. She sat up very straight, which obliged her abundant breasts to raise her dress, and at the end of the V of the neckline one could see the beginning of her cleavage, which she tried to hide with a jeweled pin. The dress seemed longer from behind than from in front. They were both near-sighted. Rubén Carretero extended his hand, and then she, Vicenta Herrera de Carretero. What names, they took all the "r"s for themselves, she thought as she said pleased to meet you.

Mondays, at 8:30 in the morning, she had class with Vicenta, who wouldn't answer a single question unless the students addressed her as Mrs. de Carretero. Tuesday afternoons she had the principal, and also on Fridays at ten in the morning, in a small classroom where she sat in the front row, right in front of him. Vicenta smiled very little, and was soft on the students. He never, ever laughed, and was tougher.

The second week of being at the school, the second week exactly, fifteen minutes before the end of class on Friday, the fourth class that she had had up to that moment with the principal, she raised her gaze from the notebook in which she was writing and found his eyes fixed on hers. She quickly lowered her eyes and continued taking notes. Pretending to take them. BAM-BAM-BAM she felt in the middle of her chest. After thirty seconds, she thought, it was a coincidence, our eyes met because I'm right in front of him, and her heart continued calmly doing its job, bam bam bam, bam bam bam, bam bam bam. Without being able to avoid it, she looked for his eyes again, and there they were. More intense now, slightly more almond-shaped. She lowered hers, and, with them fixed on her notebook, asked herself if she was seeing things. That teacher with the severe manner . . . She raised her eyes a third time, and now held the gaze. A few seconds, and the bell rang. Why had he done it? Because she was fifteen, brimming with boundless energy and imagination. Friday and Saturday she couldn't sleep, enraptured by the incident. Sunday she slept well, and woke up on Monday with dark circles under her eyes; not because of the bad nights but because she was anxious to find out if the teacher would look at her in the same way again.

Their exchange of glances grew as the days passed. Carmina developed strategies for staying within sight of the principal, in the dining hall, in the classrooms. That Friday, as assembly was ending, she was picking up her books when he came up to her.

"If you need anything, Carmina, let me know. Let me know, and I'll do what I can to help you."

It was a whisper said with the same expression on his face that he used when he gave instructions in class, but he did not address her as Miss Andrade, as he normally did.

Until a year ago she had always gone to the matinee at the Arenal with Mygdalia and Ana Rosa, but since Mygdalia had decided to meet secretly on Sunday afternoons with her boyfriend, with whom she would also sit in her living room from eight to ten that same night, the only visiting hours allowed by her father, Carmina now only went with Ana Rosa, which let Mygdalia justify her outings to her mother. During the four hours of the double feature, with a newsreel and previews, Carmina contemplated the only scene in her own private movie. She raised her eyes from her notebook and there were the teacher's eyes, fixed on hers, intense, insinuating. BAMBAMBAM, BAMBAMBAM, BAMBAMBAM. She raised her eyes from her notebook and there were the teacher's eyes, fixed on hers, intense, insinuating. BAMBAMBAM, BAMBAMBAM, BAMBAMBAM. She raised her eyes from her notebook and there were the teacher's eyes, fixed on hers, intense, insinuating. BAMBAMBAM, BAMBAMBAM, BAMBAMBAM. Her unusual muteness on leaving the theatre made Ana Rosa blurt out excitedly, when they began to walk the five and seven blocks that separated them from their respective houses,

"Hey, what's up with you today? You're in the clouds."

She kept going to the movies, more in solidarity with Mygdalia than to be entertained. She became introverted, solitary; books became her most frequent company. While her school friends talked at recess about trips to Coney Island and sweet-sixteen parties, she was silent. She became known for being too serious, inaccessible to boys. To grow in front of the teacher's eyes, she became the most sensitive of students; she graduated with honors, and was elected valedictorian. But by then she had had the abortion, and had decided to end it with the teacher once and for all.

The looks and the "if you need something ask me for it" continued until the Friday of the last week of November, when just before the last class he came up to the bench in the yard where she always sat between classes, barely shaded by a short tree, almost a bush, from which hung huge bunches of yellow flowers that she had never seen before. They told her it was from India, rare in Cuba, and they called it a *casia* tree, not acacia, and she had chosen the bench more for the history and rareness of the tree than for the shade it provided.

Suddenly, in a whisper that didn't wait for a reply, the principal told her that he would be waiting for her the following day at La Copa in Miramar. She interrupted her reading of *Oh, the Interwoven Shadows!* and asked herself if what she had heard was true. He had spoken so softly that the sound of the words was mixed with the rustle of the flowers on the casia tree, moved by an incipient north wind. While she repeated to herself automatically *Oh, the shadows of two bodies that come together*... she could see Mr. Carretero, now at the desk in his office, talking to Vicenta.

She didn't have any desire to eat that night, nor to have breakfast the next morning. She ate a little lunch, and read until late at night. He terrified her, with that big word he defined what she was feeling, the idea of a meeting. She wouldn't know what to say, what to do. The game of glances was fun, exciting, but then to meet him at La Copa in Miramar...

Her first thought, on waking up on Monday, was how nice it would have been to be seven years old, to hide under the bed and refuse to go to school. She arrived late so as to avoid the line for going into class, and during each moment of the day focused her attention on avoiding meeting up with him. She didn't understand a word of what was explained to her in any of the subjects. She knew when, where, each of his classes were, and she avoided them. She watched the office, so she could move away when she saw him enter it. On Tuesday, she didn't know if he looked at her because she never raised her eyes from the paper on which she wrote, or she pretended to, and disappeared from the school as soon as the last bell rang. On Wednesday, between one and two in the afternoon, she felt her jaw tremble when she saw him approach, even though the sun shone through the branches of the casia tree and she could feel it on her back. At that moment he should have been teaching second-year biology.

"You stood me up. I waited for you until four-thirty."

Her stutter was incoherent.

"It doesn't matter. We are birds, and we walk in the sea. Another day."

And he walked slowly back to his second-year biology class. She would have liked to go after him, to tell him to give up the game. The road she was on frightened her. She took back her glances, and she was never so happy as when Christmas vacation arrived. She spent almost the whole time at home, even refusing to see Mygdalia and Ana Rosa the majority of the times that they called her. She went around as if sleepwalking, on the one hand fed by a longing for the exchange of glances, on the other tormented by the thought of the end of vacation.

When classes began, he looked at her a great deal, more than ever if that were possible, and on Friday of the first week he announced to her again that he would wait for her the following day at La Copa in Miramar, at three in the afternoon. Like the first time, he didn't wait for an answer. The only difference was that on finishing his instructions he added:

"Don't stand me up this time."

She felt herself harassed, but defenseless to continue to negotiate. Now she did call Mygdalia, to warn her that she was going to lie by saying that she was going to study with her.

"Of course, girl, don't worry, you can count on me for whatever. I'm going to Ana Rosa's house for a little while, and I'll tell my mother that you're going to meet us there. Shit, now I finally understand why you've been so weird lately. Don't worry, not a word to Ana Rosa if you don't want her to know, but know that if you need to, you can trust me, I'll tell you that. You have to tell me, who is he?"

"I'll tell you when we see each other; come by here some day after school this week."

At five past three she was saying good afternoon to the principal, who opened the door of his car so she could sit next to him. He asked her where she wanted to go. And how the Hell would she know where she wanted to go? She had never been in a situation like this.

"Wherever you want. You pick."

He turned on the radio and began to talk about classes, about school, to talk about the other students. She didn't listen; she really wanted to pee, to run away from there, but she smiled and even commented. They got to El Reloj, on the road to Rancho Boyeros. She recognized the place because at her mother's gatherings and among her schoolmates, it was said that Americans went there to watch mambo dancers have sex. They said that they paid each one twenty dollars, and that sometimes they composed scenes—"they would say *tableaux* now," Carmina edited mentally—in which the tourists participated, and then they paid more. She didn't know how much more. They went into a reserved room—a little room that smelled of mildew, with walls covered in Formica patterned to look like wood. There was a sofa covered in black plastic to look like leather, and on one of the walls was a frame decorated with balustrades, around which wound red carnations made of dirty paper. A waiter entered and placed two cold beers on the small table in front of the sofa.

Sitting in the New York subway car that was arriving at Fifth Avenue and Fifty-Third Street, she looked at without seeing the poster about abortion designed by Barbara Kruger, and couldn't really be sure that the reserved room at El Reloj had had the decoration that she now remembered when thinking of that day. The sofa must have existed, because he lay her down on it, and she wasn't on the floor. It seemed to her now that he had asked her if the kind of beer the waiter had brought was okay with her. Her favorite drink at that time, and of this she was sure, was a malted milkshake, but she answered that she loved that beer. He took off his jacket and tie, poured two glasses, and unbuttoned his shirt. He took her face between his hands and kissed her forehead. He began to unbutton her blouse. She let him do it, thinking that she was in no way enjoying the situation, but that if she had gotten herself into this mess it was better to go on, to get it over with as soon as possible, and not to see him again. The sixth rule of her mother's gatherings and the first of her father's preachings dictated that it was better to die than to look ridiculous.

On seeing her naked, he took off his glasses, looked at her

for a long time, told her that she was as pretty as a picture, and asked her what she wanted him to do. How the fuck should she know what she liked? This was the first time she had been naked in front of a man. Her experience in matters of love was limited to kisses; they had felt her up a few times, and once a kid who said he was four years older than she was, but was actually her age, had kissed her so hard that he split her bottom lip open. The truth was that the most exciting thing that she had discovered in the field of sex was masturbation. Rubén looked at her inquiringly, waiting for her to take the initiative that she would never take. After a few minutes, he said, sticking his hand between her thighs,

"And what if I suck that sweet little thing you've got here?"

That's fine, she responded, relieved that he had decided to do something, and on opening her legs, found to her surprise that she was wet.

He kissed and sucked her for more than an hour, and she sucked him, with a revealing mastery, according to the perception that the teacher went home with. And that night while watching television he meditated on how amazing the girl was, a real cummer. In reality, Carmina put into practice stories that she had heard from her friends and at her mother's social gatherings, combined with gestures and expressions taken from the movies.

When the moment seemed right, she pretended to have a thunderous orgasm with screams and contractions. He did have one. On getting home, Carmina waited until her sister Marisela was asleep and masturbated silently until she came without a fuss.

They kept seeing each other at La Copa in Miramar. From the second time onward, they went to a room in the hotel that also smelled of mildew but had a bed, nightstands, and a bathroom. During those two years, and for several more, she had thought she loved him passionately. Now, sitting on the subway, she struggled to get inside who she had been, to understand her feelings. What could she have fallen in love with if they never carried on a conversation, if they never spent a day together, not even an afternoon, if that relationship was reduced to two or three hours on Saturdays, to fifteen minutes on the school couch one or two times a week, and to their dealings as teacher and student during class time? But for two years, his was the only skin that she pressed close to hers.

Four days after their first meeting, that January after returning from Christmas vacation, Mygdalia came to visit her. Her mother invited her to dinner, and they stayed together talking until after ten that night. It was Wednesday, the day that Marisela slept over at their grandmother's house because their aunt worked until dawn at the hospital, and they were scared to leave Petra alone in case her blood sugar should suddenly go up or down.

Mygdalia, once she knew the details, spoke with the voice of experience. It seemed great to her. Not even Françoise Sagan could have thought of something as interesting as what had happened to Carmina.

"The school principal. Girl, you really hooked one. Now what you have to do is follow my example. Listen to me carefully; let him give it to you from behind all he wants. But from here," and she placed her two hands together over her pelvis, "Nothing. This is sacred."

Carmina almost laughed, because in that position Mygdalia looked like a parody of Botticelli's Venus.

"Listen carefully to what I'm telling you, and pay attention; you can't lose your head. Do everything, except that. Preserve your virginity. Look, it doesn't matter to me that I'm Rafael's fiancée or that we're going to get married next year. He's really insisted, but nothing doing. And if something happens to him, as crazy a driver as he is? What if he has an accident, or falls in love with another girl at the last minute and leaves me at the altar? He's as macho as fuck, but what would I do, eh? Then where will I find someone who will marry me, with my cherry popped? That, you don't bring into the mix, and the rest can go to hell. Relax and enjoy it; like my mom says, that's the only thing you take with you."

She followed that advice for some months. Rubén, like Mygdalia's boyfriend, insisted. He wanted nothing more in this life than to make her his, and Carmina heard her friend's voice, "Don't bring the front part into it." But one Friday at five in the morning, waiting anxiously for Saturday to dawn, she was reading Juana de Ibarbouro's *Take Me Now, Since It's Still Early*, and she decided she wanted to "be" Rubén Carretero's. She decided it because she couldn't imagine that in the future she would want something as intensely as she wanted to feel Rubén inside her this sleepless early morning, and she thought that the rest of her life she would regret not having obeyed such a strong demand from her body.

From then on, they made love on Saturdays in the motel in Miramar, on weekdays on the couch on the fourth floor of the school, on top of a wobbly table on which, stripped of her panties and with the school uniform skirt hiked up to her waist, she lay with her hips up, the only part of her that fit on the little table, while Rubén, standing, penetrated her, and she wrapped her legs around him to avoid sliding to the ground. She adopted that precarious posture two or three days a week, when the other students were having recess. Other times they went up to that little room crammed with unused books, wooden chairs missing an arm, typewriters with missing keys, and worn-out blackboards leaning against the walls. And pushing aside the mess she climbed up on the little table to satisfy the teacher's desire and masturbate with her legs open and her knees bent as if for a gynecological exam, until culminating in the show of an orgasm that was faked there and that only bloomed at home, locked in the bathroom or after her sister had fallen asleep in the bed next to her, imagining that the teacher hugged her and told her he loved her.

He never said it. Her desire to have him say it made her devoted to Christ of the Cleansings, to whom she went to pray to every Friday after school with Mygdalia (to whom she had confessed to not following her advice), and to Saint Judas Tadeo, advocate for the impossible. In reality, her petitions would have been difficult to concede, even if the saints had the intention of doing so; because as strongly as she begged that he love her, that he feel she was inside him, that she was part of him, she also prayed for Vicenta. Poor deluded woman, she always gave her a grade of Outstanding, and as busty as she was, she was no longer a young thing, and with those close-set eyes, who was going to want her if her husband left her? And she seemed to love him so much. Every time that Vicenta came into the classroom where Rubén was teaching, she would approach the desk and caress her husband's head. Carmina, sitting in her usual seat in the first row, would decide not to see him anymore. So carrying her contradictions, she went every Friday to the chapel of Christ of the Cleansings, and every Tuesday to the novena at Saint Judas Tadeo.

She ended it with him the morning that she graduated from high school. It was difficult to do it while she was going to school. He harassed her when she tried to avoid him. Timidly, Carmina would express her needs. She wanted someone to go to the movies with on Sundays, to sit with in a café, to go to a restaurant. She was tired of these hidden games. He would respond that she should be patient, or he would walk away disgustedly, to come back a little while later or the following day to say that he would be waiting for her on Saturday at three in the afternoon at La Copa in Miramar, or on the couch in half an hour at the end of class.

She never saw him again. It was the early sixties; the government took over the private schools, and Rubén's whole family left for Mexico. About two years later she ran into one of her former classmates, who told her that Vicenta had had a son.

She got off the subway at Lexington Avenue, without having remembered the dream, but having recovered her private romance novel intact. Or who knew how much she had invented, or omitted, in this version fabricated thirty years after the events.

On returning to her apartment, she found a note from her neighbor in 4B with his phone number, that she should call him. He invited her to dinner. She had thought about having a coffee with him, but she didn't think it would be so soon. In Esashi, the Japanese restaurant on Avenue A between Second and Third, he told her that he taught film at the City University, and that he was making a documentary about undocumented Mexican workers who worked in Chinatown and didn't speak Spanish as their first language.

"It's fascinating to me that many of them learn, in a really short time, enough Chinese to communicate with their bosses and the Chinese clientele, and almost speak better Chinese than Spanish."

He had been in New York for ten years; he was Mexican by birth, but his parents were Cuban. Carmina spoke about her job; she told him she had been married twice, the first time to a Cuban and the second to a Moroccan. She thought about telling him about her daughters, their professions, about her grandchildren, but they began to talk about other things, and she told herself that she would tell him another day.

They continued to see each other in the free moments that their busy lives allowed them. One night, two months later, he invited her to his apartment for a glass of wine.

"Are you inviting me to have a glass of wine and that's it, or do you want me to go to bed with you?"

He looked at her, surprised yet smiling at the directness of the question.

"To bed seems perfect, if you want to, of course. I've wanted to sleep with you since I saw you in the elevator and saw the charm around your neck."

"Then let me go to my apartment to get my electric toothbrush. I can't stand to get up in the morning and not have it."

When she returned, Darío said to her,

"You know what? What I like most about you is that I feel like I've known you forever."

The bedroom, illuminated by the weak light from a small nightlight whose dark crystal shade bore the face of a woman in a hat, smelled strongly of Champa incense, but since this was her favorite the smell pleased her. The room's two windows, set into a melon-colored wall, wore white lace curtains. By then in bed, Carmina thought that if she had seen the room without knowing the owner, she would have sworn that it belonged to a woman.

Darío was soft and decisive, spontaneous in giving and taking, and patient in waiting for her, which made Carmina happy, since, like the general in *Arráncame la vida*, she firmly believed that in this game the end is what's important. On the edge of falling asleep, feeling that she was sinking into something so soft it couldn't possibly be a real mattress, a photograph on the dressing table caught her attention, though she made it out poorly in the dim light. An old couple sat on a flowered sofa, both with glasses, the woman's eyes a little close-set. And then she dreamed the same dream as two months ago, but in the morning she remembered it completely.

It's a clear, sunny day, but not hot. About three in the afternoon. I walk, I walk, I walk, and while I'm walking I think about how good it would be to see this man again. I don't want to go to bed with him; I want to talk, to have the conversation that I never could before, to talk about what really interests me, to say what I want. I feel really good thinking this, but the trip is very long. I get lost; I think I'm going to be late for the date if I keep walking. I decide to cross the lagoon in front of me, swimming. I'm getting to the shore. On the other side of the lagoon, on a bench under a small tree, almost a bush, from whose branches hang huge bunches of yellow flowers, a man is sitting waiting for me.

She awoke before he did, thinking of the dream. How good it would have been to have had a conversation with Rubén, but she was sure that train had already left. However, the fact that she had made the decision to talk in the dream consoled her. If she saw him, she really would be capable of doing it. Distracted, still not very alert, she turned her head and saw the photo of the couple. She got up trying not to make a noise, took the picture and observed it closely. BAMBAMBAM. BAMBAMBAM BAMBAMBAM. It wasn't true. She went to the window and lightly pushed back the curtain, until light came though a crack. She looked at the photo slowly. It was them, twenty, twenty-five years after her high school graduation. Rubén and Vicenta.

Darío was sleeping. If they handed her a book at the publishing house with a story like this, to accept or reject for publication, she was sure she would reject it. Who was going to believe a story like this? She smiled. How good that this was her life, not fiction, that she didn't need anyone's approval to continue her story. She looked at Darío and understood the meaning of that chain of coincidences. She had complained so vehemently, on so many occasions, that life had never given her the chance to tell Rubén that she loved him, that now it was being offered to her in his son. How would he take it? Was it fair on her part to make him a participant? What would he feel for his father? And for his mother? It would be easier to be silent; she had done so up till now. More intelligent, her mother would have said. She concluded that it was her responsibility to herself to tell.

When Darío woke up, he made coffee. It was Sunday; they had the whole day to themselves, and sitting at the kitchen table, she asked him about the colors of the bedroom walls and the lace curtains. He smiled, took a long drink.

"Everyone asks me about it. I don't really know very well myself; the only explanation I can find is that it was a reaction against my father. He was really good to me, but he made my mother suffer so much, with all the women that he always had around, that I identify with her in many things. We're really close. I think I had a ninety-nine percent chance of turning out gay, but instead I ended up having feminine taste, according to traditional norms, for home decorating, especially in the bedroom."

"Tell me about your parents."

"They were Cuban, like I told you. They had a school in Havana; when the government took it over in the early sixties, they left Cuba. My mother was pregnant, for the first time after sixteen years of marriage, so I was born six months after they got to Mexico. She wanted to give me my father's name, but he insisted on Darío. She never understood his whim, but she accepted it because it was her habit to please him, much more than he deserved, I think. Now that I'm older, the explanation my mother invented seems very interesting to me. I'm sure she came to believe it, and it's the one she still tells friends today to justify the choice of my name. My father never affirmed or denied it, and I saw him smile on various occasions while she was speaking, which knowing him, makes me suspect that his decision had nothing to do with my mother's theory. As much as he admired the Nicaraguan poet, Rubén Carretero was so macho that he was even proud of his name, because, according to him, the repeated "r"s were a symbol of masculinity. He was embarrassed that his taste in Modernist poetry should reach the extreme to make him want to name his son after its greatest representative. I tell you the old man was a real nightmare. Just after they got to Mexico they opened a bookstore, and we always lived off of that. They never taught there. He worked until he died last year, and she's still living in the house they bought in Coyoacán right after they arrived, and where I lived until I left for New York.

Carmina looked at him fixedly and imagined that, given the opinion he had of his father, what she was going to tell him wouldn't affect him too much. She began slowly and with effort, because there are stories that, when the events that made them have died, resist being resucitated, and even reject the words that name them. But she had to speak. She had to.

"I knew your parents, and I studied with them in the school they had in Havana."

He stopped drinking his coffee. She spoke for fifty minutes, and he didn't interrupt her once. She told everything, just as she had remembered it on the subway two months before. Even her desire to name the child she never had Darío. Then she was silent. He shook his head, as if scaring something away.

"Wow. That's incredible. Do you know that would make a great movie?"

As the last word of the story left her mouth, Carmina felt that she had touched the bottom of that cloudy lagoon whose blue tinted water she had carried deep in her soul for thirty years, and that with each sentence spoken that morning she had managed to open a floodgate through which it had emptied. And the sensation of feeling clear water filling the space inside her that had been occupied before by stagnant water was almost physical.

They spent the day together, and at night went to see an Aranda movie at Anthology Film Archives. On returning to the building they said goodnight before he got off the elevator at the fourth floor. Each of them had to work the following day, so they slept in their own beds. He didn't invite her over again, nor did he call. She left two messages on his answering machine, and then stopped trying.

A month later they met up again in the elevator. He greeted her pleasantly, mentioned the heavy rain that day and commented that his mother would be coming to visit in two weeks, but by then he would have already moved, to a larger apartment he had found on the Upper West Side. Carmina smiled at him when they said goodbye at the fourth floor, and continued on to the fifth. She walked the hallway to her apartment thinking that she would have liked to say hello to Vicenta, she had really liked her, and as she turned the key in the lock, shook her head.

She made fried rice with the chicken left over from the night before, made a salad with lettuce and a whole cucumber, dressed it with extra virgin olive oil and seasoned rice vinegar, poured herself a glass of red wine, and put on an Amalia Rodrigues album. And she murmured to herself as she ate, moving her shoulders to the rhythm of the *fado*; who would have thought to tell her thirty years ago that thirty years later she would spend such a good night and have such a good conversation with Darío, Rubén and Vicenta's son.

❋ The Deepest Seed of the Lemon ❋

(1997)

Good and evil are what we value and fear.
And, however, what we value and fear
Is only within ourselves.

—*Tao Te King*

"Martirio. Martirio, I feel bad. Martirio."

"What's wrong?"

"I feel really bad."

Martirio extended a clumsy hand towards the reading lamp, overturning a glass on the nightstand. She turned on the light and squeezed her eyes shut. "Shit," she said when she saw the spilled water and looked at the clock. Four a.m. She turned over and made an effort to open her eyes. Sitting on the bed, Rocío looked at her expressionlessly from behind her messy hair, her image reflected in the mirror of the dresser in front of her.

"I feel bad."

"Bad physically?"

"No."

Martirio shook her head, trying to wake up.

"Did you bring the pills for headaches? I've got a splitting one. You remember what my mother was saying this afternoon, that sometimes she wished she could take her head off and put it away for a while and put it back on again after the pain had passed? That's how I feel now."

Martirio walked sleepily to the dresser and took two Tylenol out of her purse.

She held the glass of water as the girl, shaking, drank. Now awake, she returned to her space in bed and watched the girl's trembling chin and hands as she brought a cigarette to her mouth. She took a match and lit it. Absorbed, she watched the faces of the little bears sitting on the *cachumbambé*, printed on the T-shirt she had brought as a present and put on that night as a nightgown, slowly grow wet. The bears are placed exactly over my breasts, she thought, since they need to collect the tears that fall every time I wear this T-shirt. And she watched how, from their little smiling wet faces, the tears slid down to the writing at stomach level: *Friends Forever and Ever*.

The sobs, and the prolonged whimpers after them, brought her out of her abstraction. She should say something, but she didn't want to speak. Not after the argument that afternoon. Since she arrived three days before, there had been a series of uninterrupted disagreements, to which she really hadn't paid attention, too focused on her happiness to see the city, her friends, to be with Rocío; but the argument this afternoon had been *too much*, a jump into the absurd, into silence.

"Who are you for in the Gulf War, the Americans or the Arabs?"

It was in the Habana Libre, which was no longer called "Libre" since one Spanish company and then another had bought the hotel. The untimely question, out of context, hurled as she flourished a drumstick of fried chicken in one hand, provoked the feeling in Martirio that the girl on the other side of the table had touched a computer key that opened an old document that she wasn't looking for. At the time she didn't understand, and in the minutes that it took for Rocío to chew and swallow the chicken she had in her mouth, she remembered an anecdote that she had read as a child in *Reader's Digest*, when the magazine seemed to her the greatest, since its pages contained the only pleasant home interiors that she was able to contemplate. A woman who was extremely upset by her own timidity had been advised to take a class to improve her general knowledge, so she would have more to talk about in social situations. She signed up for a history course, and months later, sitting in a restaurant with some people, one of the silences that made her so anxious occurred. After some minutes in which nobody spoke, she looked at her dinner companions, one after the other, and when they were still silent, she began to drum her fingers on the tablecloth and said, "Isn't it terrible what happened to Marie Antoinette?"

"I'm not for either of them," Martirio answered. "It seems to me like a perfectly savage mess."

"Well I'm for the Americans."

"And why?"

"Because they were right to attack. The Arabs disobeyed the United Nations."

"And you think the United Nations has to be obeyed."

"Of course. It's an international organization."

"Then why don't the Americans obey the *overwhelming* majority decision of the United Nations—which almost every country, with the exception of the U.S. and two others, has voted in favor of for years—and lift the embargo on Cuba?"

From behind her messy hair, Rocío demanded her attention with her gaze. She looked at her.

"But can you explain what's wrong, or do you not know?"

"I do know, but I'm afraid to say it."

Martirio leaned back against the wall that served as a headboard for the bed and closed her eyes.

The girl took a deep breath and stopped crying.

"What the Hell, I'm going to say it. And whatever happens, happens."

She took a sharp drag on her cigarette, and with insecure fingers, pulled two or three tobacco fibers that had come out of the filterless cigarette off the tip of her tongue.

"It's that I slept with someone, with a man, even though I promised you I wouldn't. His wife suffers from asthma. I thought I could be faithful and monogamous, but I can't. I've realized I still like men, that I can sleep with them, even in a nice way."

She accompanied the sound of the word "nice" with a movement of her arms away from her body, palms upward, that reminded Martirio of a flower opening.

"Besides, it was a really sad situation. I was hungry and didn't have anything to eat, and he went and looked for the only thing they had for lunch at his job, a plate of plain spaghetti, and he brought it to me."

Huge sobs overtook her again, long moans.

"He's like me, and he gave me his food."

"What do you mean by, 'he's like me'? That he lives here?"

"That's right. And because he lives here, sometimes he's hungry and he can't find anything to eat, and he likes meat and when he doesn't eat it it's because there isn't any. And he never has any, and it doesn't even occur to him to become vegetarian, because he is one out of simple necessity; and he's never tried broccoli in his life because he's never seen it. He doesn't practice yoga either; first because, like me, he thinks it's a piece of shit that has never been part of our culture and that it's only good for entertaining people who don't have to stand in line all morning, rain or shine, to get a hard roll that's going to get bitter two hours after they give it to you and a miserable piece of ground tofu that sits like a stone in your stomach when you eat it because the kind of soy beans that they mix with scraps here is the kind that they grow to feed animals, not for human consumption, and it's been scientifically proven that it was largely responsible for the neuropathy epidemic we had here and that a lot of people are still suffering from, including my mom, even if you say that's not possible. Tofu, listen to me well, is disgusting. That's what it is, disgusting; and if you dedicate yourself to preaching about its benefits when you come here for a week, it's because you bring dollars to eat breakfast, lunch, and dinner at the hotel buffets where I can't go because I don't have anything like what those meals cost, and if I find a foreigner who invites me, I get set upon by the security guards for being a *jinetera*. And if you can get up thinking about doing yoga for two hours and worrying about maintaining your muscle tone, it's because you don't get up asking yourself if that day you're going to be able to take a bath when you're dying of heat and flush the toilet when you take a shit, if you have a toilet, and because you know you're going to have water and light in your house every time you turn on the tap and every time you turn on the lights. And even if I wanted to learn yoga, until recently I wouldn't have been able to, because here they've almost thrown out really talented people once they discover they practice yoga at home. Now things have changed a little, but who knows if one day they'll go back to how they were before. How can you trust anything in a country where a television schedule comes on when they begin to broadcast and then nothing they put on has anything to do with what was on the schedule? In addition to all these things, he's like me because he thinks that like De Gaulle says, the only thing worse than one communist is two communists, and he believes the Bay of Pigs was invaded by Cubans, not by Americans, like your little journalist friend told me that night when we were having coffee in New York."

Roció fell back, exhausted. Her breath came in gasps, and her trembling hands tried unsuccessfully to light the cigarette that had gone out between her fingers.

Martirio felt drained. Completely. She sat down on the bed, slid one leg to the floor, then the other, stood up, and barefoot, walked slowly to the kitchen. She pulled two squares of paper towel from the roll she had bought with dollars the day before, opened the refrigerator and poured two glasses of mineral water from the bottle she had bought along with the paper towels, because she was afraid of getting sick if she drank tap water. She returned to the bedroom in the same way, gave one of the glasses to Rocío, calmer now, and placed the other glass on the nightstand. She began to mop up the water that had spilled when she woke up, thinking as she did so, observing that the moisture had formed a white stain on the varnish of the surface, already damaged before getting wet, that she would have to pay the owner of the apartment to repair it. With the lighter she had brought as a gift, she lit the cigarette that had gone out that Rocío held between her lips.

Resting against the wall again, Rocío smoked now. Martirio sat on the other side and drank half of the water she had poured herself.

"And if you feel so bad here, why don't you leave? You've received an excellent education, studied something only rich people can afford to study in the United States, as you yourself told me once. Your English is pretty good; you just need a little practice. You'd get a job easily."

"Yeah? And how am I going to fix it so that I can go up and down the subway stairs and walk the thousands of blocks that one walks there for anything with this arthritis? How do I work out the issue of transportation? No one's going to feel bad for me because I'm lame, and I can't drive a car. And anyway, I would have to depend on the subway, because there's no way I'm going to leave here to go to Oklahoma or one of those places in the country. Not even to Philadelphia or Boston. If I left, it would be to go to New York. Here, I live in Havana, not in Bejucal or Güira de Melena; in Havana, which, in spite of how run down it is, is a great city. And what happens when I have to go to the doctor, I, who have to go to the doctor every other minute? Yailín got bronchitis when she was over there, and she came back saying that getting sick in Cuba is almost a pleasure, but in the United States it's really unfortunate. I couldn't believe it when my cousin, the one you met in Brooklyn, told me that four days in the hospital for a c-section cost fifteen thousand dollars."

"Maybe your cousin can help you. You can stay with her while you get on your feet."

"The night that I had dinner in her apartment I asked her, and she said that well, maybe it would be okay for a little while, because she lives with her husband and son in a studio, but that's not a workable solution for me. They spent all the time talking about how hard life is there, and I think they said it to discourage me, because they told me about twenty times that I would have to look for a job right away. I told them of course, on taking a step like that, the first thing I would do when I got there would be to look for whatever spot of work I could find, because at first I won't have papers. But the truth is that if working all day and getting home at night with no desire to write is a condition for living there, I'm staying here, because writing is the most important thing to me. And what about my mother? I can't leave my mother behind. First, because she'll die of sadness if I do the same thing our father did to us; second, because I don't know how she's going to live. How's she going to get by with the 177 pesos she earns a month, eight dollars when she exchanges them? And the third reason is that I don't even know how to fry an egg. And look, even if I did have it all worked out, I don't know if I would be able to put up with that piss they call coffee over there, or their fucking obsession with not being able to smoke anywhere. As if people didn't die over there anyway . . . Listen, and if you, who sleep with me, didn't offer to let me stay in your house, why is my cousin going to?"

"Because you didn't tell her, like you told me, that you like to be waited on, and that you were used to having everything done for you. You've seen what my life is like; I can't afford to be with a person who doesn't work but expects that I, who am up since five in the morning, will come home and make her coffee, instead of waiting for me with the coffee pot on the stove, ready to make it for me. But I appreciated your frankness in telling me this, believe me."

"That's why I say what people want to hear."

"But if you feel bad here, but you don't want to leave either, I don't know what you're going to do."

"Nothing, fuck it, absolutely nothing. Do what I do; try, however I can, to live as well as I can.

"I haven't told him I'm gay."

"Why?"

"Because he's a conventional man. And his wife suffers from asthma."

"That's the second time in half an hour that you've mentioned his wife's illness. Is it that she can't fuck? What I least understand about what you've just told me is why you've hidden the fact that you're a lesbian. I thought you didn't get into those games. After all the stories you've told me about how you couldn't even consider a monogamous relationship, about having ended your relationship with Julio, who, according to you, wouldn't have cared if you'd slept with a woman or a nanny goat, now you've hooked up with a troglodyte to whom you can't even admit who you are? That's inconceivable to me. Not only inconceivable, but disillusioning, in the most exact sense of the word. What I loved about you was your frankness, which I considered your courage in a social milieu in which the ability to dare to be openly different from the majority is almost unknown."

"I already told you that when I meet someone I try to look as good as possible, and I knew that you were going to like hearing that. I think the whole world is like that. I've also never told you that I've spoken badly of you. I don't know if that's going to bother you."

"Why have you spoken badly about me?"

"Because in New York I hated you and I loved you, sometimes at different moments and sometimes at once, but I never told you."

"I never felt that way about you. In spite of the arguments, we had such a good time; we did so many things together. And in bed? Don't tell me now that you didn't like those little movies, because it was your idea to rent them, and you looked like you were having a great time watching them. We even agreed that the best one was the fat woman with the two guys. I wanted to bring you a postcard I saw with a picture of her nude, or almost nude, wearing nothing but one of those belts that she uses in the movie, but I didn't have time to look for it."

"Deep down, I wanted you to change," said Rocío, watching the cigarette between her fingers, now almost down to the end. "You didn't want the same thing from me?"

"No. I wanted you to not want me to change."

"I would have liked to kidnap you and tie you up and force you to eat what I ate, to smoke, to forbid you to eat broccoli and tofu, and to make you forget about yoga."

"And why did it bother you what I did? Every day you were there, you ate a steak with fries or fried chicken with fries. It didn't bother me that you ate whatever you wanted to. I thought that you were happy, and I think that you were."

"Are you going to hate me for having slept with that man?"

"Not for that."

"I was hungry."

"But you came back with six hundred dollars, and that was only three months ago."

"I bought the television. Have you forgotten? I told you I was going to buy it. I'd never had a television in my life, nor had my mother."

"And you spent six hundred dollars on it?"

"Almost five hundred. My mother didn't want such an expensive one, but I swear, I don't know anyone who has a better one. And anyway, the remote was sold separately, and that was another fifty."

"But the living room in your house is so small that there

aren't even three feet between where you sit to watch television and the TV set."

"That's true, but we only realized that after we had bought it, and they wouldn't give our money back.

"Are you going to sleep with me again?"

"I don't know. Not right now, no. This should have lasted that month, like I suggested."

"It's true; you were right. More experience."

"Why didn't you tell me what was going on, how you were feeling, on the phone? We talk every week. I wouldn't have made plans to come for so long, nor would I have rented an apartment to be with you. I would have stayed with my family like I always do."

"You came to work, not to be with me."

"For work, I would have come for a week. I planned to be here three weeks for you."

"Well then, stay here in this room the whole time, without going out."

"You're crazy. I want to see the city, the pier, the moon. I thought we would do it together."

"I hate the city, detest the pier, and abhor the moon."

"The moon too?"

"Yes, I'm a very resentful person. And if I didn't tell you anything, speaking in all cynicism, it was because I needed you to come so you could take me out to eat, and so you could bring me the computer cables I left."

"Then why didn't you shut up so we could have spent these days peacefully?"

"Because I couldn't. I tried, but I couldn't get it out of my mind, and I couldn't stand to see you happy, and that's why I fought all day. I'm an imbecile. You're the best relationship I've had."

"I'm the best relationship? Why?"

"You always understand what I say, even if we never agree, and you know how difficult it is for people to understand me. Julio, for example, never understood; and in the end the problem was that I was more intelligent than he was and he didn't want to admit it. And women . . . if you knew what kinds of women I've been with. Once I went out with one just because I liked her tits. A week."

"The problem is that the tits have a name, sweetheart."

"Are you really going to hate me?"

"Not for that. I would really resent it if you slandered me."

"I talked with my mom this afternoon; I told her everything. She thinks it would be better if I went home tomorrow."

"If you prefer it . . ."

"Are you going to give me the vibrator, like you promised?"

"Sure, you can take it with you tomorrow."

"Not that. And what about you? Leave it for me when you go, just don't forget."

"Don't worry, I almost always do what I promise."

Martirio looked at her watch. It was already five o'clock.

"Let's sleep a little while. I agreed to meet with two writers at 10 a.m., and I'm going to be dead tired."

Martirio turned off the lamp, covered herself with the sheet, and curled up her legs. The air conditioner, its thermostat broken, was mercilessly cold, and there was no blanket in the apartment, and she hadn't brought one because why should she imagine that she would need one? She thought about turning the machine off, but she had done that the night before and she woke up sweating. She couldn't sleep if she was hot. She closed her eyes.

Rocío put out her cigarette in the ashtray next to her, and as she adjusted her head on the pillow, Martirio heard her say,

"You're very good. The truth is that thinking it over, the way I ended up sleeping with that man was strange. You think that because he brought me . . ."

"You're not going to tell me that story in detail, right?" Martirio interrupted, opening her eyes without moving from the position that she had adopted to try to fall asleep.

"It's that you're so reasonable."

"Telling me that story strikes me as an enormous lack of feeling on your part. Anyway, you already told me. You were hungry, and you slept with a man that brought you a plate of plain spaghetti."

"No, no," exclaimed Rocío in a rapid gesture, sitting up in bed and waggling her index finger in a sign of negation.

"It had tomato sauce."

She met her one afternoon in a used bookstore in New York, Martirio told Marta Veneranda; maybe it was early summer. Yes, early summer at a literature conference in Havana, seven years after having ended what she thought would be her last relationship. Tired of mutual misunderstandings, she put the same passion that she had once put into relationships into meditation and yoga, and now lived calmly, contentedly, considering herself lucky to possess a past that was an almost inexhaustible source of stories and to which she attributed a large part of her productivity as a writer.

Rocío came up to her as she finished reading one of the stories from her most recent book, and asked her directly if they could speak together alone some time, before she left Cuba. The insinuating way in which she fixed her eyes on her with no shyness reminded Martirio too intensely of old gazes, of her adolescence in Havana, to refuse, and she invited her to have lunch with her the following day, Saturday, at noon. She was returning to New York on Sunday. As the girl walked away, Martirio observed her uneven walk. Back in the hotel, taking a shower, she thought that that look had taken her back to a time in her life that she hadn't visited in years.

On reading over the menu, Roció observed that she had forgotten that beef existed; what's more, she thought that having lunch in itself was an activity that belonged to the past.

Sitting that night on Gladys's porch, Martirio, touched, repeated the comment to her childhood friend.

"It could be true that she hasn't seen meat in a long time," affirmed Gladys. "But she doesn't remember what it's like to have lunch? . . . Please, Martirio, the girl was *jineteando*, just looking to get a meal."

Upon saying goodbye in the restaurant, after seven at night, Rocío gave her several stories, asking her to please read them. By that time, Martirio already knew that Rocío's father had been an incurable ladies' man, as well as given to seeking employment in occupations looked down upon by any society, but even less acceptable in the one in which he found himself. On abandoning, in 1980, both the country and the women, large and small, that depended on him, he condemned them to a life of poverty and to humiliations that left permanent scars on the body and a hidden bitterness, greater than the bile of any living creature, on both their souls. The damage to her body was apparent; the damage to her soul Martirio only discovered later. The worst calamity, said Rocío, was feeling obliged to give up acting, her primary vocation, when the symptoms of arthritis forced her to accept that an arthritic actress would be seriously limited in her choice of roles.

She had a boyfriend, a nice guy, but she also frequently went to bed with women. In fact, she had had two relationships with girls. Her mother knew about it; they had talked about it. She wasn't sure she liked the idea of a bisexual daughter, but she accepted it.

Martirio returned to New York impressed by the maturity of that child able to overcome misfortune and, as they say in English, to make lemonade when life had given her lemons. Above all, she admired her honesty, her lack of duplicity in telling her personal story.

She didn't think about Rocío frequently, but on occasion, while she waited for the subway or as she returned home from one of the workshops she taught, there arose in her a feeling of calm happiness at knowing she was in the world. That was all; she didn't feel an urgent need to call her, or to know about her life. It was good that she existed.

When, in October, Martirio served on the organizing committee for a conference on literature, she put forward Rocío Linares Ballester's name, and the young writer arrived a little before Christmas.

She went to meet her at LaGuardia airport, and in the taxi that took them to her house, where she would stay, she told her that she had bought her some sea cucumber and glucosamine pills with chondroitin, that were said to really help arthritis. On entering the apartment and seeing Martirio take her suitcase to the guest bedroom, she said, before she could put it down,

"I'm going to sleep with you. I broke up with Julio. I don't think I'm going to sleep with a man ever again."

Martirio smiled at the emphatic declaration, and got out an extra pillow so she could lie next to her. It was snowing lightly. She turned off the bedside lamp so Rocío could better see the falling snow, lit yellow by the light of a street lamp.

In the almost six hours that she spent in the three airplanes that brought her back to New York, plus the waits in the airports for connections, seventeen hours in all, with the exception of a few hours of sleep, Martirio meditated on the episode with Rocío and on all her previous relationships. Seventeen hours is a long time.

She was so tired of crazy people. So incredibly tired. And she saw herself ages ago, the after-dinner beer bottle empty, listening to Mark's amorous joys and sorrows. And she remembered the night of a full moon when she had wanted him to hear her confessions, and how he had refused to listen to them, saying it wasn't worth it to relive the stories of past loves. She remembered Ada's crazy jealousies, her weak act of love, the night that she chased her around the house with a knife, on coming back from studying for her master's exams with a friend from school, who was married and in love with her husband. She saw Diana throwing tomatoes, lettuce leaves, radishes, cucumbers, the whole salad out the window because she had had lunch with Ada six months after ending the relationship with her ex-lover. She remembered Consuelo's incurable need to comfort every woman who crossed her path—in bed. She remembered Silvia, for whom she was always guilty until she could demonstrate her innocence one hundred percent, and even then she was never convinced. She even thought about Shrinivas, whom she had only been with a weekend, but hey, he'd made her suffer quite a bit by being so good for two days and then disappearing from her life forever. And now this last one, Rocío, lying and slanderous. Her mother would have said that the luck that she'd had would draw tears from a stone. She would have said it was a fucking mess.

It was true that the circumstances of Rocío's life would have been enough to unbalance even the most even-keeled. Where had that phrase come from? And Mark? His problems came from the Korean War, and Ada had been completely messed up by her childhood in that school run by nuns, where she was forbidden from wearing patent leather shoes because her panties would be reflected in them. My God, how much foolishness could fit into the human mind when it came time to raise children. And Diana's stories made one afraid. Martirio, whose childhood had lacked everything except maternal love, felt herself short of breath on imagining her ex-girlfriend accosted by a mother whose religious fanaticism forced her to live obsessed with Hell and to watch over her daughter mercilessly to keep her away from sin. Consuelo was the most justified. She got along perfectly for having grown up in three foster homes and having been abused in all three of them. And Silvia came to the United States with Operation Peter Pan, and floated from orphanage to orphanage for a year until her parents got to the United States.

But shit, her own childhood as the daughter of an Andalusian refugee from the Spanish Civil War who came to Cuba six months pregnant, without a cent, mourning her murdered husband, hadn't been the most pleasant or safe either. There was a reason her name was what it was, and she'd suffered plenty, and she'd almost died of sadness after her mother's suicide attempt. "Well," she sighed, sitting in the cafeteria in the Cancún airport as she bit into one of the chicken sandwiches that she considered the most delicious in the world, "Because I come from where I come from is the reason I've spent my life with that string of crazies."

A few minutes before landing at Kennedy airport, her eyes closed, she saw Rocío's upset face during that absurd argument, her rage, and felt that, having wanted the opposite, absolutely the opposite, she had pushed out the deepest seed of the lemon that misfortune had planted in the girl's soul. Every morning, before squeezing the lemon she had cut in half, the juice of which she would mix with water to break her fast before drinking her coffee, she would carefully take out all of the seeds with the point of a knife. She would dig section by section, in search of the most hidden ones. When she was sure that none were left, she would squeeze it. However, sometimes with the last drop of juice a seed popped out, and on every occasion that she saw it, she told herself that since it was the deepest and most reluctant to come out, it must be the bitterest at the core and the tartest at the center. And she asked herself, if it had the chance to sprout, would its shoots have the same qualities? She never tried it. She limited herself to searching for it in the glass with a spoon, and when she took it out, to observing it for a few seconds before depositing it delicately in the trashcan. So much effort, even if it had been in vain, deserved recompense.

She understood why the lemon seed popped out; it was a question of pressure. If you squeezed hard enough, it had no choice but to come out, no matter how deep it had tried to hide itself. As she buckled her seatbelt for landing, she asked herself if she had unleashed the bitterness in Rocío. Maybe, she told herself, I pressed hard enough, without wanting to, on her button of desire. "But how much it hurts to hurt," she thought as the plane touched down, and she felt happy to be back. In a health magazine, she had read that everyday, on waking up, she should think of three things in her life that made her happy. On reading that, the first thing that came to mind was New York.

She paid the taxi driver, picked up the light, almost empty suitcase, and entered her building thinking that the only image of Rocío in Havana she was going to hold onto was that of the first night when she arrived, when they made love before that rancor began to froth. After their caresses, on coming out of the bathroom, she saw her sitting on the edge of the bed with her face buried in the bathrobe she had just taken out of the suitcase. She would remember her hair, as she saw it on opening the bathroom door, dark and silky, and her answer when she asked her what she was doing,

"This bathrobe smells like you. It smells like New York."

When she thought of Rocío in the future, the rest of the images would be of Rocío in New York. Rocío dazzled by Times Square at night, happy to cross the Brooklyn Bridge on foot, joyful at seeing paintings she had admired for years in the pages of books for the first time in museums, posing smilingly for that pencil portrait on the sidewalk on Broadway, satisfied at taking hundreds of pictures to show her friends when she got home, excited as she picked out erotic movies in the video store. She would remember her watching them naked, her legs open, sitting on the couch in the living room, asking her to make her come, that those scenes made her really horny and she couldn't wait. She would remember her sitting on that bench on Sixth Avenue after midnight, singing in a low voice a song Martirio had been so surprised that she knew. *I want a Filipino handkerchief and a necklace of coral, and a little chain of gold and a blue stone from Portugal. I want . . .*

❈ Life Leads ❈

Lord, give me a merciful heart
in the face of all human suffering.

from the liturgy of the mass.

. . . the forced march of life
pushed her forward.
Not without a bitter pain

—*"Life leads" by Ofelia Rodríguez Acosta*

My way is *carpe diem*, Martica, open your eyes. Living in the moment and not worrying about what's going to happen tomorrow, that's how I've been able to survive, and this philosophy is what keeps me from committing suicide or leaving the country. Leaving . . . no way. People change a lot when they leave, and in spite of all the shit I have up here, I like myself as I am. Especially the eyes. I've never understood why, but when they come back they won't hold your gaze. Here we look at each other, and we forget how long we've been looking at each other, but people who live outside, I don't know what happens to them, but they won't meet your eyes. They don't walk the same way either. The other day I was coming back from the funeral for Roberto, Tati's father, and it started to rain and on the other side of the street I saw Rubén, that guy who studied with me in La Lenin, walking in the rain, and I thought that if he lived outside he wouldn't walk the same way, with that same easy stride. I don't know, these might just be crazy thoughts of mine, but it seems to me that getting wet in the rain here is not the same as getting wet in the rain somewhere else. These might just be crazy thoughts of mine.

What you can't do is give up . . . in short, you never know; you get lucky, and in one minute your life comes together when you least expect it. One minute of clarity is enough. Look at me; who would have said a year ago that I would be living as I live, as fucked-up as I've always been, Martica, with the house key hung on a string around my neck from the age of four so I could come and go as I pleased, Mommy singing in those clubs until three or four in the morning, and the old man going from meeting to meeting, so you never knew when he was going to show up. And now I have dinner waiting for me when I come home, the bed made, clean clothes. I have everything I never had when I was little. And look at how it all worked out. In the craziest way ever, at least from outside. From inside, it happened in the most logical way, like it always happens. A Puerto Rican woman who was at school with me always said that we learn everything by hearing it: the only one who knows what's in the stew pot is the spoon that stirs it, and that's how it is.

You've tried many times to figure out what the change in me is due to, because it's true that I'm like a different person; and I've brushed you off, so as not to tell you. I've changed the conversation, I've acted like a crazy woman. You know it. Well, look, if I haven't told you, it's because our lives are so different now that I almost feel embarrassed to tell you. But it's not because I don't trust you, it's not that at all. And today I decided that I'm going to tell you the whole story. The whole thing, because if I don't talk I'm going to explode. Look, I needed to talk to you so much that I even came here by bus. The tire on my bicycle got fucked up last night, and since it's Sunday there's no way to hook up with Yoluis, the only one who can get the part the bicycle needs. The only one. But he goes out hustling on Saturday night and he won't get home today until seven or eight in the evening. And I had to talk to you. I waited for the bus for more than an hour, friend, with my saintly patience. It took so long to get here that I was already singing like Elena Burke: "It's ten to two, it's ten to two, if the bus doesn't come, I'm sure I'll walk." I don't know how I can still be in the mood for jokes. Speaking seriously, you're the only one I've thought of telling this to, the only one I'm sure won't repeat it to the first person to walk through that door after I leave. Because, sister, people in this country are so gossipy. Martica, is it the same over there, where your mother lives?

On the way here I was thinking about all the shit we've been through together. Do you remember the night I hooked up with the Spanish guy, the one I'd said no to about five times because I couldn't stand him, so you, Jacinta, and I could eat? I went out to look for him in that crazy downpour. Don't make that face, girl, that was a fucking long time ago. Do you remember when I hadn't seen you in two weeks, and you opened the door for me with the baby stuck to your breast, that didn't even seem like your own skinny breast, and the little girl was crying because she was sucking and nothing was coming out? And you with the huge circles under your eyes that made you look like Dracula's bride, and me without a red cent, so I'd gone to your house hoping to find something to put in my mouth there. I immediately thought of the Spaniard, because I'd run into him again on the street that afternoon, and he'd hit on me again.

I almost can't believe how you've dedicated to yourself to the girl since she was born, and to Armando since you've been living together. But believe me, it seems great if that makes you happy, and anyway, you're even plump, which in your case makes me more than happy. But please, listen to me quietly, even if I'm repeating stories you've heard a hundred times, and when you hear what I've come to tell you, don't say, like I've heard you say to people who've told you stories recently, that there are limits, that there are things you don't do, lines you shouldn't cross. Don't give me all that, because we've known each other too long, and I'll just get up and leave. Crossing the line. I also have lines I don't cross; I too have my limits. I'm not going to have kids so I can hang a house key around their neck when they're four years old so they can come home at eleven or twelve at night when they don't have anyone left to play with in the street because the whole neighborhood has gone to bed, and, after sitting alone next to the door waiting to see if mom or dad will come home while they're still awake, they go to bed alone, and are alone until someone comes home at three in the morning.

It's true I'm high, but if it weren't for this high, I wouldn't be sitting here. It must be the weed Tamara brought me. I don't know where she gets it from, but every time I smoke some of Tamara's weed it's as if I swallowed a parrot. I, who barely speak, you know how I am. And this loquacity is pure weed; I swear I haven't touched coke in more than eight months. And it just happened that she brought me some today.

Don't freak out, I'm going. The thing is that at the time that I was walking around with the house key around my neck, my mother was a singer. I know you know this, but be quiet and listen to me; that's the way it has to be if you want to find out. Cabarets, restaurants, parties they hired her for; she even did radio programs. But the one who was going to change my diapers if they couldn't hold another piss, or fry me an egg, or open a jar of Russian jam after I'd screamed myself hoarse from hunger, was my dad. My old man, the poor guy, he tried; but he spent his life going from one place to the next. One day sent to Camagüey, the next needed in Pinar del Río, he almost never spent a night at home. And when Mom was there, she was rehearsing or talking to her crowd of gay and lesbian friends. That's why it's so strange that that mess, as the Puerto Rican girl called it, should have happened between Olema and I.

I couldn't stand the repertoire that I had to put up with at those rehearsals. At one point she was into Spanish songs.

Can you imagine? It was the worst. Indigestible. By this Conchita Piquer, a name that no one of my generation has ever heard mentioned. They repeated those fucking little songs so often—and I hated them so much—that I couldn't help but pay attention to them, and I ended up learning them by heart. What do you think of that? And I still sometimes find myself humming them, and when that happens I bite my tongue and ask myself if deep down I really like them. What's the worst is that many of the things of hers that I rejected I now realize that, after all these years, I've made them mine. "To the lime and the lemon, I have no one who loves me, to the lime and the lemon, I'm going to end up alone." There was another about a whore who falls in love with a foreign sailor that has a tattoo of a woman's name. The cheesiest lyrics ever written, but there are mornings when I wake up with it in my head and there's no way to make it go away: "He was beautiful and blonde like the beer, his chest tattooed with a heart." Them singing their shit, and me with the house key hanging from my neck watching them from the corner without opening my mouth, but hoping that lightning would strike them all to see if my mother would pay attention to me. They called me the little mute, and this made me angrier still. I sucked a pacifier until I was seven and drank milk from a bottle until I was nine. Those were my comforts, the only ones until I began to fuck. From then on, that's been how I resolve all my problems, physical, economic, and emotional. I've been fucking since I was twelve. I began so early I doubt that virginity even exists, because I don't think I ever was a virgin. The first time they stuck it in I didn't have any of the things I'd heard my friends talk about having had. Blood? Never. It almost didn't even hurt . . . just a little. Why should it hurt, if boys had been sticking their fingers in me every time we were alone together since the fourth grade? At first they had short fingers, but as I began moving up in grades their fingers got longer and they kept sticking them in me. I don't even know why I let them do it. After I fucked myself over with that infection, when I met you that week in the hospital, the psychiatrist there said that I grew up with impoverished self-esteem. Impoverished, what a ridiculous word. He was truly impoverished, even his butt cheeks were impoverished, and after such a to-do and so much shit analyzing my behavior, one day he showed them to me. But I didn't let him touch even a pubic hair, and truly, it's never bothered me if they touch them, or even if they keep some as a souvenir. Laugh if you want to, but I once went out with this guy two or three times, I'm sure it wasn't more than three, and months later I ran into him again on 23rd Street, on a day when I was fainting from hunger. You don't remember this story? The guy invited me to a restaurant called Rápido, and as soon as he sits down to eat, he takes out a cigarette case he'd inherited from his father, a famous cardiologist here in Havana who left in the early sixties, promising him and his mother that he'd send for them as soon as he got recertified, but he never did and he never sent for them. And the only thing he left his son was the cigarette case, and the unhappy guy grew up with it and treated it like a treasure and kept souvenirs in it instead of cigarettes, according to him, although once in a while he kept a joint in it. Well, what do you know but in the middle of the hamburger I'm wolfing down, because I've been living for three days on tea and custard, he pulls two or three little curly hairs out of the cigarette case and says they're mine. Since the hair on my head is straight, I realized right away where they were from, but I kept on eating, serious, so he'd stay calm. I wanted to finish eating and run out, because the guy was in the mood to unload and I wasn't up for that. He closed the cigarette case with all the solemnity you'd find in a Saturday evening movie and I, so as not to wind him up, was left wanting to ask him at what damn moment had he pulled out the pubes and what right did he have to hang onto them. I suspect he pulled them out of his mouth when he had it down below; it's the only possibility. How fucked up that they even hang onto your pubic hair.

When I started pre-university, the old man had already split and at that time I began dating the only boyfriend I've ever thought about having a stable relationship with. Stable. I must have been crazy to think it, since I don't even know what a stable relationship consists of. The two of us went on some benders where we woke up with both our faces stuck in the same vomit, without knowing who had vomited or when. We got along well. We fucked whomever we had a mind to, together or separately. We went out at night looking for people in some of the scummiest bars in Central Havana, and we picked up some incredible people. We had a good time. It didn't matter much to us if they were men or women, fat, skinny, old, young, with teeth, toothless; the thing was to have someone to fuck. We went with them to a little room Miguel Gabriel had over by Santo Suárez, so tiny that he and I almost couldn't fit in it by ourselves. Well, there we squeezed everybody in, on top of an old mat that ended up in flames, it took on such a foul stench. Things got ugly when, after doing two guys at once too many times, I got some hemorrhoids that put me in the hospital for five days. Streams of blood every time I sat on the toilet. What a scare, Martica, I don't want to remember. Shit, I had . . . a fucking hard time of it. Up till today, no one's been able to stick even a finger in my ass. All it's good for is shitting, and well . . . During all this, I was living with Mom, and with all the trouble she had and everything, I was in the second year of University, in the College of Humanities. After the hemorrhoids, I developed a little bit of ill will towards Miguel Gabriel, since it wasn't the same anymore. I began to feed his obsession by putting another man in the bed, because that's what he liked most of all, the scenes of ecstasy that we played out. And I thought that what was going on was that he was a huge fag, but because of some kind of repression that he got who knows where he didn't dare fuck a *macho* without having me in the middle, to give himself the idea that his fagginess was part of the game. But the ass that got fucked over was mine. I think his must be made out of rubber, because he used it quite a bit too, but what happened to me never happened to him.

After that episode, I didn't see him so frequently. I didn't see anybody much, truthfully. I became disenchanted with everything. I love that word. Disenchantment. To become disenchanted is tremendous. That was when I developed a taste for being alone. All in all, the only thing that people bring with them is a fucking mess. I even got good grades that semester. And that's with doing everything for myself because Mommy . . . for unreliability, she can't be beat. But since life has always sent me one problem after another, one afternoon Olema showed up at my house. I didn't know then that her name was Olema. Standing in the doorway of the main door, I almost couldn't make out her face, something I'll never forget, because my mother's house faces west and the sun was setting and the afternoon light shone behind her and shadowed her face, looking at her from where I was, sitting at the dining table, the only table in my mother's house, writing. I see her as if it were now, standing in the door: a countryish looking girl with a beat-up suitcase in one hand. That's how I met Olema. She said she was from Pinar del Río, and that her father was my father's uncle, because her grandfather had been old when he was born. We asked her to come in, and she said she'd been born near the Valley of Viñales, a really strange place. She and a pile of relatives lived perched on some hills, without electricity, and they healed themselves with water. I don't know if they were related to the cures of Ana Moya, the people from Regla my grandmother Estrella belonged to, who also healed themselves with water. Olema decided to come to Havana because she got tired of the dark. Poor thing, she didn't know . . . My mother then told her that she should go look for my father, but I liked her eyes so much—it was her eyes—that right there I told my mother that she knew full well that the old man's new wife wasn't going to take her in. She could sleep with me. Olema had a kind of desolate look, the look of a person who's seen a lot of sad things, of a person who's suffered. But her eyes were free of the late-night, hangdog exploits that I saw in mine when I looked at myself in the mirror in the morning. I liked her eyes. I liked them. And I hung onto her like a tick so she would want me. And she wanted me, and we began to make love in the bed where I slept in my mother's house; and for some months I didn't go out with anybody else, because I didn't want to, because the only thing I wanted was to be with Olema and read. I acquired a great love of reading when I stopped spending my nights sleeping in vomit. But life has always been ugly with me, I'm telling you. Suddenly my mother started getting under our skin, calling Olema and me dykes, and she began to make our lives impossible . . . impossible. And she began to speak badly about us to the relatives perched on the little hills over there in Pinar del Río. And there I was trying to get Olema to start studying, because she's really intelligent, but she didn't have any peace even to think, with the fights with the old lady. And she started saying that we were pigs, that we weren't just two women, that we were also relatives. Can you believe such gall, to become such a moralist; she, who had raised me listening to the greatest indecencies you can imagine. I'll never forget a story that they told in the days when they were rehearsing Conchita Piquer's songs, about a lady friend of the group who was said to have a clitoris as long as a finger. Have you heard of a more terrible thing to say in front of a small child? It's true that I didn't make myself noticed because I almost never spoke, but there I was sitting in a corner with my pacifier in my mouth, and I wasn't invisible. Well, things went from bad to worse until one night at two in the morning, as Olema and I were on the point of getting off together, the old lady shoots like a racecar into the room, shouting so loudly that the whole block heard: out, out of this house, Satan-spawn, because she'd found religion and was now singing in a church. And she put us out on the street in the middle of a drizzle, the kind that you almost can't see but when you look at the street lights it seems like there's a small curtain in front, the kind that chills you to the bone. That was what happened to us that night.

To make a long story short, because it makes me feel so bad to remember it that I can't make it long—it's enough not to be able to erase it from my brain—I'll tell you that when Olema and I separated, almost two years later, there was no difference between her gaze and mine. At the back of her eyes you could see the same hangdog expression that you could see in mine. I don't know why she came down off her hill.

We spent almost two years on the streets, sleeping in parks, in the train station. When it rained, we looked for someone who would let us sleep in their house and give us a plate of rice and beans in exchange for a little girl-on-girl action while they watched. Days without bathing; our friends ran from the horrible way we sometimes smelled. I think they felt bad at seeing us so fucking down and being unable to help. Sometimes they let us spend one or two days in their houses, but it wasn't possible to stay longer. They didn't have anything either, and anyway, we weren't easy. We became bitter, prickly; we would insult anyone over anything, we mutually insulted each other. We fell really low, it's true. In the morning, we would wake up from the bad night—because we never really slept fully asleep, for fear that something would happen—and we would go off to look. For whomever, a tourist, someone who would pay to squeeze a tit, for a blowjob under a stairway. We would eat a custard, have some tea, and I would go to the university—because I was still going to the university—and Olema would wander around the pier, through the parks, take a siesta in the alleyways of Old Havana, until we met up in the afternoon. She was almost always waiting for me with food, and sometimes with a few pesos. She would say that she had gotten them from some friend, or by showing a generous tourist around. I would eat what she had brought, and on some occasions there was even enough to pay for a room for the night. That was the best; we could love without eyes over us. Sometimes, with a little money earned this way, she would catch a bus and go to Pinar del Río to see her family. She missed them, especially a little sister that she had cared for from the time she was born until she left home. I would go wait for her at the bus station the day she came back. There were times when I waited for eight hours. I always tried to meet her with flowers and something to eat. I generally brought her *mariposas*, which I bought fresh and sweet-smelling, but which, as the hours passed, would wilt, and my heart wilted with them, I swear, for the things I'd had to do to buy them. And when they were no longer white but that half-transparent caramel color petals turn when they wither, the bus would arrive and I would give them to her, and Olema would be happy about them, and that made me love her even more. And it didn't bother me that she shared her cunt with other people, because she had to really love me to say those old flowers were pretty. She didn't ask where the food had come from either, but I always explained, some tourist I accompanied, you know how they are, they have money and they don't mind paying well when you act as a guide, or I had cleaned a house, or who knows how many lies we told each other that neither of us believed. Because we both knew that tourists—male and female—give money to be sucked, and more if they can stick it in.

Then, on one of her trips to Pinar del Río, I caught that horrible infection and ended up in the hospital, where I met you, giving birth to Jacinta, who up to now hasn't wanted to change her name, as I thought she would as soon as she learned to say it. Because listen, I know how much you love that novel of Galdos's, I also like how the guy writes, without caring about the opinion of those who think they know better because they don't drink cheap wine, but to go and name the little girl Jacinta . . . I know you can't stand invented names; you weren't going to name your daughter after a city or a continent, because you can't stand that idea, and let's not even mention your name, not even think about it. It's true your mother went too far, leaving without saying goodbye. Shit, mine didn't either. And to become vegetarian over there, where meat is plentiful, and to make herself famous telling other people's forbidden stories. I want to see when she's going to tell hers; let's see if she dares to one day. But you have to admit that she didn't have the bad taste to saddle you with her whole name, because that Veneranda is plain shitty, and it very well could have occurred to her and you wouldn't have been able to do anything to avoid it. At least Marta Eugenia sounds like a queen. I actually like it.

I got out of the hospital and went straight to wait for Olema. The bus arrived at noon, according to the timetable, but I got to the station at three in the afternoon so I wouldn't have to wait so long. I still didn't feel very well, and that day it almost happened that she got there and didn't find me. At 3:05 there she was getting off the bus. I had absolutely nothing in my hands. I did have, now I remember it, a little flower I'd picked on the way. Yellow, spindly, I think it was one of those ones they call "flower of the dead"; I don't know much about flowers. I recognize mariposas because I love them. She was shocked at how bad I looked. It was December; she had brought some tomatoes from home and she took one out of her backpack so I could eat it right there. We started walking and I felt so bad, so fucked over, that I didn't have the strength to keep lying. When I finished the story of my infection and the hospital, she told me we couldn't go on like this, we weren't going anywhere, and we were going to die if we didn't do something different. She was talking and crying, and her nose began to run and I began to cry too, and we cried so much that when we had reached the end of the road to nowhere we were on, the only handkerchief we had, hers, was all wet. Mine had been thrown away in the hospital; they said it was disgusting and a source of germs and the only thing it would do for me would be to make the infection worse.

"I'm not going to be with a poor woman ever again," she said. "I swear. There's no one who can put up with this. I'll look for a foreigner, a Martian, a Martian woman, whatever, but with money. And if I'm going to hustle, I'm going to hustle in earnest."

I looked at her eyes, and they were hard. And I couldn't believe they were stuck in the same face that had held those eyes from two years ago, when she stood in the doorway of my mother's house with the sun behind her. And I looked away, because I didn't want to see her eyes like that, because I could see the slimy puddles we were stepping in on the street in them. And I didn't look at her straight again that day, because I didn't want to remember her that way, but rather how I saw her the day she came to my mother's house. And later, when we were no longer together and I walked on aimlessly feeling horrible—because in truth it never hurt so much to separate from someone, I thought that what had happened was that a huge rain had fallen before Olema arrived, and I saw in her eyes the image of the puddles that were really in the street, that remained etched in mine each time I took my eyes from her face and looked down in the middle of that devastating conversation. But in any case, I didn't look at her any more, because it fucking hurt to see her so sad and I couldn't do anything and I felt like I was going to faint; I didn't know if it was from the weakness left over from the infection or because we were ending it.

We did resolve the situation, at least momentarily. She met someone who was almost a foreigner right away, and I hooked up with a real foreigner. Olema's was a Cuban woman; she worked in tourism, in an Italian company, and got paid in dollars. Almost a foreigner. Mine was Spanish; he didn't live here, but he came every three or four months on business. He would spend a few days with me, and would leave me money to live on until he returned. A good guy. He had a wife and son in Barcelona, but he fell in love with me. I think he fell in love with how well I fucked, because in truth I made a real effort, but I made an effort because I liked the guy and I wanted to stay with him. He even once proposed having a child with me, but I wouldn't go that far. You know my theory about limits, and I know myself. And look, it would have really suited me . . . When he wasn't here, I led the life I led since I broke up with Miguel Gabriel, with the exception of the time I spent with Olema. Most of the time shut up in the house, listening to music, reading, writing, scribbling, doing nothing, until one day when I don't know, something gets into me and I go out and hook up with someone at the movies, or ride my bicycle, or I go into a bar in some neighborhood far from my house and sometimes I stay there three or four days. I do it once in a while, not a lot. If Antonio was in Cuba, we were always together, unless he was working. He never looked into my life away from him. I was incredibly lucky, because he wasn't even old; he looked great. A little plump, but nothing more than a little. He even bought me a cell phone, as expensive as they are. Before coming, he always let me know he was coming. But once, he didn't let me know, and he found me in the middle of a scene that ruined my life, with a giant fat woman with spiky hair, half-punk, that I had picked up in one of the bars I went into. It was fate, a difficult destiny that I've gotten stuck with, I'm sure, because it was the first time I'd gone out in more than a month, I swear,

Martica. The truth is that the fat woman looked like—no, not a fireman, she seemed like a wrestler. And in addition, she had made it a condition on going with me that we bring her girlfriend, a skinny bottle-blond with a mouth painted a shocking red, whose bones you could count one by one. God knows what shitty illness had her so stripped down. But I wasn't thinking about anything. I tell you, I don't know how I've made it this far. That's why it seems like I'm really sane now, without caring what people think. Well, in the middle of that mess, coked up to my eyeballs and drunk as I was— because if I hadn't been I swear I wouldn't have gotten into that, I hear the key in the lock, and I freeze. But what could I do. In effect, Antonio. Standing stock-still in the doorway, he contemplated the spectacle with an expression not of rage, nor of surprise, but rather of tiredness, a great tiredness. He looked fixedly, his eyes expressionless, and I didn't know what to say. I became so nervous that I asked him if he liked pastries. I asked him because he wasn't saying anything and I didn't know what to say, how to move; I didn't even dare move to reach for a shirt and throw it on. And the women, naked, stayed in the same position they had been in when the door opened, paralyzed, until I felt bad when I calmed down because after all, I was the one who'd picked them up at the bar and had even insisted they come with me.

Antonio answered slowly, as if I hadn't been participating in the scene, that the only pastries he liked were the ones he bought at the pastry shop, and even those he rarely ate lately because he wanted to lose weight. He grabbed the suitcase he had set down, closed the door gently and left, I imagine to go to a hotel. So. I didn't even move to tell him to stay, although I was dying to do it, because I knew it was useless. What I did do was throw out the fat woman and the skinny one in an instant. Daughters of bitches, especially the one with the punk hair, to have made me take along that wash-up she went around with, and I was such a shit that I agreed. What bad luck. The only time I'd gotten myself into something like that since Antonio's last trip to Havana, I swear. I ended up so low that in the following days I crawled instead of walking. I went on hands and knees to the kitchen when I couldn't take the hunger any more, opened the refrigerator and took out anything I could toss into my mouth. Antonio came back about three days later. He wasn't condemning my lifestyle, if that made me happy, but he couldn't deal with it. Then I did cry; I begged, I insisted I was happy as it was. It was the loneliness, craziness, what do I know, anything but happiness, please don't say that. He already had enough emotional baggage in Barcelona, with a wife who wasn't easy and an adolescent son hooked on drugs, and now here I was, he said, and I never saw him again.

Without money again, without a phone, without a way to pay the rent on the apartment where I had lived since I began seeing Antonio. To go back to sleeping in the park, no. I couldn't conceive of it. The nastiness, the infections, the rats walking over me. No. One night they ate a toenail; another night a cockroach bit the little finger of my right hand. People say cockroaches don't bite. They do bite; they bit me. No way, no. Although I had graduated from the College of Humanities, it didn't occur to me to look for work. What for? In the midst of all the shitty plans I hatched to resolve my situation once and for all, the biggest shit occurred to me, the great shit, and it worked. Go back to my mother's house. But I couldn't go back to battle it out; I had to find a way for her to love me, to look after me. And since the only people she really looked after were her lovers, I would be her lover. Just a little fuck once in a while, of course I could. Can't you see that I know her well? She was retired now and fucked, most of the friends she had gotten together with to sing Conchita Piquer now dead and gone. The thing wasn't improvised in my head in that moment. When she went on the attack with Olema and me and threw us out of the house, she, who never minded, on the contrary, who liked to go around with people who fucked whomever, the crazier the better, why this attack? My conclusion was that she became jealous.

The only safe house I could count on was hers, so I presented myself at the door one afternoon, with some tamales that I'd bought in the street from a woman who made good ones. I bought a few beers and smoked a joint before going. All things considered, what maternal relationship had we ever had? It's true that it was very strange the first time I had my face between the legs from where I had come into the world. She could never imagine what I thought in that moment. I thought that when I was born I had had my face in the same place I had it now, but in the opposite position; I had been leaving her, and now I was entering her. And if you knew, I might be crazy and it doesn't bother me, but that idea made me feel better. Look, it's all a question of turning a situation over and reflecting on it. I have friends that live at home like

I do; their mother does every thing, like mine does for me now. They're more dependent on them than I am because my situation is clear; I warned the old lady that once in a while I was going to disappear for three or four days but that she shouldn't worry. Think about it; it makes sense. She knows I'm never going to leave and not come back, first because at this point I'm convinced I'm not meant to be in a relationship with someone who demands what I can't give, and I'm not going to see myself on the street, and second, because I'm her daughter, however you want to put it. Of course there's always going to be some little fuck-up, and when I don't come home to sleep, as soon as she sees me—but in a nice way, gently, so I don't get upset, which is incredible if you compare it with the past—she says that the food she left on the kitchen counter covered with a plate so flies wouldn't get it went to waste because I didn't eat it in time. But I don't pay any attention to her. I don't say anything to her because I hardly ever say anything to her now, but I think there were plenty of times when I asked for something to eat and she wouldn't even look at me, and back then I couldn't get it for myself.

And now they've almost stopped talking about it in the neighborhood; there almost isn't any more gossip. Can you imagine? Everybody fascinated by the fact that I was there, that I was taking care of her. I'm the prodigal daughter. The truth is that it's the first time in my life that she's taking care of me, that she makes me beans like they're supposed to be cooked, thick and everything. My Puerto Rican schoolmate would understand this, because there are some things you have to know from the inside. These days it's occurred to me for the first time to look for work in something related to the degree that I finished while hustling. Of course, since I've resolved the problem of a house and food. So anyone . . . It's silly, to understand that, you have to have seen yourself sleeping on the streets. Do you know what it is for the first time in my existence to have my mother hug me when I ask her to, to have her hug me without my having to ask, to have her ask me to hug her? If I had the courage to write this story down, I swear I'd get rich. That's what a German guy I hooked up with one night at the Copacabana told me. I told him a lot of things, because he was leaving the next day and he didn't even know my name. I told him it was Alana, because that's what I would have liked it to be and so the name would be prophetic: *ala*, wing, flight, and because he was going to fly and I would never see him again. Who knows if the German guy was right, but people like morbid things, just look at the success of your mother's stories. But I would never do that; I'd die before I'd put my old lady's name on everyone's lips, because no one knows what she's been through. Listen, she hung a house key around my neck when I was four, but her mother left her in a field five days after she was born, and if the old Asturian lady who raised her hadn't found her quickly, the ants would have eaten her. It took her more than two weeks to get over their bites. And then, she and the old lady all alone. They went hungrier than a pair of stray cats. If it weren't for the little songs she learned and the cabarets that she sang in from the age of fifteen on, I wouldn't have even had a house key hung around my neck, because I wouldn't have been born. I don't know if that would have been better or worse; what I know is that I'm here, and to Hell with lines and limits. They can all go to Hell, and I'm already talking like her. I don't even feel the slightest bit guilty; I feel that for the first time in my life I have what I was supposed to have.

Don't look at me that way; it makes me feel bad. Fight if you want; I'd actually prefer that. Tell me I don't know any limits, but don't look at me that way. Let's make some coffee.

You know, thinking it over, Jacinta isn't a bad name; it's good to be named after a flower. I don't think about Olema often, but a mariposa flower reminds me of her without fail. And today on the corner where I waited for the bus an old man was selling mariposas and I don't know how I remembered that ten years ago today I saw her for the first time, with her beat-up suitcase in her hand, just down from the hill. Who would have said then that she was going to marry an Italian and even live in Europe. The thing is to look for the other side of things. When I was little, I hated my name, Obdulia, until my mother told me—now that we have long talks—that she gave it to me because I was born on Saint Obdulia's day, and the labor was so difficult she thought we would both die, and that so we would live, because she really wanted me to live, she promised the saint to give me her name.

Don't look at me that way, Martica; it makes me sad. Shit, now I've told you. Let's put some sugar in the coffee.

About the Author and the Translator

Sonia Rivera-Valdés was born in Cuba. Her book *The Forbidden Stories of Marta Veneranda* was awarded the prestigious Casa de las Ámericas Award in Havana in 1997. She has published short stories and essays in the United States, Latin America, and Europe. She currently resides in New York where she is a professor at York College. For more information, and to read articles and interviews with Ms. Rivera-Valdés visit www.editorialcampana.com.

Emily Maguire has translated the work of Ángel Lozada (Puerto Rico) and Javier Bello (Chile). She currently lives in Bloomington, Indiana, where she is an assistant professor at Indiana University.